PAS DE DEUX

PAS DE DEUX

TIMOTHY ROESSLER

St. Botolph's Press

New York, New York

For Tania

Inge

It is opening night. The ballet troupe whose posters had been up on all the kiosks in Cologne for three weeks, a poster with two dancers silhouetted against a black background, the man holding the ballerina lightly and carefully, as if he had trapped a bird, the ballet is finally to be performed. *Petrouschka. Giselle.*

I hover in the corner, backstage, ready, in Stadt Theater, zipping up the back of the prima's white satin costume; each of her vertebra stand out separately.

Someone laughs far too loudly despite the rigorous hush; everything should be quiet backstage. He's joking with the other dancers in the corps de ballet, flexing and bending his legs at the same time. Long and lean like the rest with a broad clown's face. Then everyone takes their places for the performance under the blue lights.

The opening notes play on the other side of the heavy red curtain, muffled, but carrying with it a marzipan fog that smothers the sighs and rumbles of the audience. The scent of the dancer's make up and the perfume from the girls blends in with the pungent sweat of underarms: herbs and vinegar. The music, the air heavy with scent, the blue lights, the ragged rows of dancers poised to enter, all of it surrounds me, makes me forget, sweeps me away from my stupid little life outside the theater—my mother, her boyfriends, my brother Kai—and the curtains swing apart, the stage lights wash over the boards. The boys and girls stand in groups of threes and fives, ready at the edges of the drop scenes. They arrange their faces, the boys equally pretty with rouge, eye shadow and lipstick, enter on their cues, sweeping out with carefree gestures. The audience applauds from their seats in the swollen darkness.

As I take my place at the props table, I pass the *prima*, a cigarette in her mouth, lightly swearing at the chief costumer who tries to arrange the bow at the back of the ballerina's peasant dress. The prima casually tosses the cigarette aside, the costumer jumps back, and she makes her entrance, and again, the audience ripples with applause.

My safety pins, threads and needles are carefully arranged in rows, ready for me to repair any of the costume. From here, I can watch, stage left: the lift and arch and pulse of the arms and legs of the dancers measured and ruled by the conductor's baton. On stage, the prima meets the prince, and she is radium and quicksilver in his arms. Upstage, I can see the boy who laughed, the muscles of his thighs molded by his tights, the impossible hump in his crotch from the dancer's belt. He royally offers his arms to a ballerina beside him, and they dance their peasant dance behind the lead couple, the toes of the ballerinas thumping on the stage. The lights fall into his eyes, jade under the black helmet of his short dark hair.

Between the frenzied sessions of slipping the girls from peasant clothes to court clothes and back again, straightening the jackets or the bodices, I try to watch him. He has a funny face, with such a small nose set between the wide-set eyes, his full lips set into a big smile or drawn into a line above the pointed chin.

The first act ends, the leads take their bows, and the rows of ballerinas swarm over the back stage, each with a tear or a rip or a hole in the gauzy skirts, in bodices, ribbons undone. I lose track of him.

Too soon, the second act begins. The scene changes to a cemetery, the fog machine sends smoke over the feet of the spurned lover and the prince and the spirits of the ballerinas. They seem to curse you and become visions, even to me at my table. Three boys are stand behind me, whispering, and again the same one laughs. When I turn to frown at him, I see that he's making fun of the lead dancer, mimicking his movements and the too-romantic expression he wears on stage.

Dawn comes with a pink spotlight, ending the ballet. The stage manager hands the principal a bouquet for the prima, the audience claps, the curtains swing to and fro. The musicians pack up their violins and trombones, the audience files out, leaving a trail of twisted programs, and I go to the dressing rooms to and arrange the costumes. Once finished, I go back to the stage to sweep. The lights are back on full and white throwing the stage into sharp relief, the tape marking the position of the sets, the tombstones and the huts, tucked away to one side, the drops raised, exposing the crumbling red brick wall at the back of the stage.

As I lean a broom handle against the wall, the boy who laughed comes up to me in his street clothes and asks if he could have a cigarette, please, in a heavy accent. He takes one from the pack of Marlboros. I light it for him, and he inhales, closing his eyes.

Did you like the ballet? he asks.

Yes, I liked it very much. I wish that I could have watched it more. Seen it from the audience.

Doesn't matter. Didn't miss much—is a shitty company, but it's work. Are you an actress?

No.

That's good. Dancer?

No.

That's good, too. But you are beautiful enough to be one. Prettier than the prima. Look, it's not much of a compliment—lots of lizards are prettier than she is. Here walk a little.

Yes, he says, as I stroll back and forth, blushing, you carry yourself very gracefully. You're really not trained?

No.

Why are you here, in the theater?

I want to be a costumer.

He looks blank.

Clothes. A wardrobe mistress.

Do you speak English?

Yes, but . . .

Good.

He smiles, waiting for me to say something.

Where are you from? I ask, in English.

Moscow, then Toronto for a little bit. Then New York.

But why are you dancing with a company from Rotterdam?

Myself, I don't know. I ask myself that same question every day.

It must be wonderful to see so many places, just like that. To live in New York. And travel around.

It's overrated. Mostly it's boring. Little tiny stinky dressing rooms. Cold studios. You don't see much. Holland especially is boring. Have you been many places?

Only to Holland. Once to Denmark.

Holland is bad—as bad as Deutschland. Denmark . . . I don't know. Good dancers from there. Do you know Peter Martins?

Who?

Doesn't matter. May I ask you your name?

Inge

Inge. That's nice.

And yours?

Alyosha. Like in Brothers Karamazov.

Dieter, one of the stagehands, waves at me, pointing to his watch.

I have to go back to work now. I add, for no reason, Sorry.

Arbeit macht frei. May I, he says in German, may I invite you for a coffee tomorrow?

Yes. You may invite me.

Would you be so kind, *genaidege Fräulein*, as to join me for a cup of coffee?

Yes. There's a nice place close by, the Rosenherz Café.

Around three o'clock?

Yes, I say. Yes, I'll be there.

Lyosha

Sleepy round faces, drowsy square heads. Drinking beer in the green light from the stained-glass windows. Waiter goosestepped over to take my order. Old and stiff enough to have served with the Nazis. Even his questions sounded like orders out of those thick lips. And the beefy guys at the bar, growling out their jokes. Worse than Russians, let me tell you, even if they shower more often. Too clean. Too big.

Brought over my drink and made me pay immediately. Girl was already late, which is bad because you have to move fast, blitzkrieg, especially on these short engagements. Not a second to lose.

She came in, looking better in the afternoon light. If that was possible. All golden hair and creamy curves. No angles. Caught her eye and then she smiled, then she remembered not to, instead to be serious, *comme il faut*.

It's easy with cash in your pockets and stories to tell. Do the talking and make them laugh, especially the Nordics, because that's what they never get from Klaus, Hans, or Heinrich—a simple joke once in a while.

She ordered a beer too, a little common, girls should stick to champagne or wine. But beer is the national beverage. And if they drink, it makes everything easier.

Talked. Chatted. Lit cigarettes. Went through the repertoire. She fell for it, this glamour that everyone but dancers thinks that dancing has. Little stories about this city or that town, Americans are like children, Canadians are like the Swiss, only more boring, and did you know about. But. As I rattled on, I noticed. Long lashes framing blue eyes the irises circled with kohl. Her small pink ear when she brushed back that sheaf of blonde hair, her full lips glistening slightly as she pulled on the cigarette, the shadowy cleft between her breasts, breasts that trembled under the black silk blouse when she laughed. And I wanted her. Simple as that.

Inge

It seems, during the ballet, that every girl in the corps de ballet needs something from me, and wants it that second. As I replace a flower that's gone missing or repair the torn tulle, they appraise me with hard, cool glances down long noses. I stitch yet another seam on another leotard. The girl stares at me directly with large brown eyes.

He's completely crazy, she whispers.

Who?

She laughs. Your new Russian boyfriend. She leans in, now intent.

Seriously. He's a total, certifiable lunatic. You should stay away from him. Anything more than a fling is trouble. I know.

Why are you telling me this?

Shit! My cue!

She flies away in panic.

It's late before I reach home. In bed, I close my eyes that are full of the shifting dreams I have seen on the stage, the corps de ballet in barbaric scarlets, blues, greens, a riot of cloth that I mend and pin, sew and stitch, tucking and fitting on this boy's shoulders or that girl's waist. The stage lights burn into my retina, leaving glowing ghosts of themselves, reappearing as I close my eyes, now in bed. The music, too, replays its jagged rhythm although all is quiet outside.

But suddenly, not so quiet. Something's pelting against my window; someone's throwing stones, and down below, amplified by the narrow courtyard, echoing giggles and shushing sounds.

I peek through my curtains just as another hail of gravel rains against the glass. Down in the gloom four figures—no, three—rummage in what must be bags but look like denser shadows. The one who'd been throwing the pebbles looks up. It's Lyosha.

Out of the bags come a violin and a guitar. The guitarist strums a few chords; the violinist tunes up. Alyosha cues them, they play a few lines of a familiar tune, then he bellows in a voice that manages to be loud, scratchier than the violin and out of tune, a song in Russian,

Oichii chornaya . . .

Then in German:
> *When the moon is low*
> *When soft breezes blow,*
> *I will hold you tight*
> *In the hush of night;*
> *We will find our love,*
> *While the stars above*
> *Will be shining in your Blue Eyes.*

He sings this—to me—over the caterwauling fiddle, as the lights snap on around the courtyard, as I laugh: in my little courtyard someone's actually singing to me. Trash and shouts pour down on them.

Gypsies, my mother hisses at my shoulder. Why are those filthy thieves making their racket here?

I can't believe it, I manage to gasp.

I can. They're simply looking for a way to sneak in and rob us. Or to see who's not home so they can come back and steal at their leisure. I'm going to call the police.

Someone already has, I say.

In the distance, sirens were already making their two-tone whine under the rough music from the courtyard. The gypsy guitarist, more alert than the others, pokes the fiddler with the end of his guitar, nodding at the gate, signaling that they need to get out. The fiddler ends the verse with a flourish of his bow. Alyosha makes an elaborate dancer's bow directly to me.

Do you know them? my mother asks.

No.

I think he was bowing to you, she says, dryly.

Inge

I wait by the backstage door, away from the light that leaks from it when it's opened. It's better if everyone doesn't know, because the stage hands, the theater workers are terrible gossips and I want at least this secret before, well, if not before but if anything should happen between us. I'm not some ridiculous groupie, some little girl that wants to sleep with the stars. No.

The dancers leave in groups, their voices tinkling against the far off sounds of cars passing on the other side of the theater, traipsing off like flocks of butterflies down the alley, some of them looking at me curiously from the corners of their eyes, but never pausing to say hello. The gray door swings open again, and Alyosha steps out, squinting his eyes to see me. I walk up to him.

He takes my hand in his own hot hand, the calluses on his palm rubbing across my skin. We stroll down the alley, then he stops, faces me and leans into me, suddenly, his mouth on mine, gently and gracefully; when he draws away, my lips follow his for a moment. He embraces me, and I reach my hands around him, my hands reach under his leather jacket, to his slender and strong his back, the muscles defined, and I remember the ballerina's back too. He kisses me again, his tongue in my mouth and I close my eyes and everything is black velvet and soft fire, and the lingering smell of his scent—yeast, leather, tobacco—blends with the scent of my own perfume. His hand slips under my coat and caresses my sides; I arch my back to press into him. He draws my hip into his and I can feel he is hard already. His mouth moves from my lips to kiss my throat and ears.

It's cold here, I whisper.

He clears his throat and says, There are two boys in my hotel room.

We can go to my place, I say, You know where it is.

So we walk, arm in arm, stopping every few steps to kiss while the evening breeze ruffles the leaves of the linden trees above us.

Lyosha

This girl, this Inge. She's all Germany to me, blue Baltic eyes, eyes of alpine lakes under clear Bavarian skies. Gold glowing hair down to the waist, like Siegfried's fire or the color of Dresden by phosphorous night.

To have her hair in your hand, wheat and barley strands like beer in the glass. It would burn if it passed through your mouth; it scorched me where it fell. Over my lips.

The first time. In her bedroom. Peach cleft wound below the crucifix on the wall, hung by her mother and the poster of David Bowie, vampire thin, staring at me from the blue. Then all lips and thighs, sea salt on my fingers. The slippery sweat over sliding stomachs. Hips in my hands, broad, ready for the swing, and her hair the fields of wheat, now gold, now silver in the light from the street lamp outside the window. My ear still listening for the mother to come in and stamp me to death under square heels. Finding me with her daughter. Who doesn't care, lost, she shifts under me, we trade places, and I'm under her, the sheets sliding against my spine. Her nose disappears, her mouth, her eyes, until only her hips are left, riding me as if I'm a mount for a Prussian, for a Junker, the thudding rhythm, riding off to Poland and pogroms through forests of firs and. . . All over. Gone and away across the fields. The pull of milk and silk. Finished. But she clings. At rest.

Cigarettes trace orange peel curls in the air. Smoke plumes drive over damp bodies. Cup the breast in the palm and suck it swollen into my mouth.

Barks from below.

Teutonic syllables: *Wer ist da?* Inge said.

Mutti.

Mommy's back.

Doors open and close, the footsteps down the hall.

Schläfst du, Inge?

Jetzt, nein.

Steps stopped at the door. No fucking closet, no wardrobe, no space beneath the bed: trapped.

Gute nacht, liebchen.

Reached for my pants. Then her hand on my arm.

Wait, she whispers, wait.

Inge

When he buzzes the door, he is already forty-five minutes late. Mother and Kai, my brother, rise from their chairs in the living room when I open the door. He strides in, with neither wine nor flowers, and kisses me on the lips while mother watches.

I take him by the hand and present him to mother, and to Kai, who looms behind her. She takes Alyosha's hand, glancing from his face down to the worn blue denim pants, the wrinkled red shirt with the seams coming apart, taking in the leather jacket.

I believe dinner is ready, she says, shall we go and take our places?

After straightening her gray skirt and patting the silver blonde braid coiled around her head, she leads the way to the dining room on the right. Kai draws back the oak chair for mother, looking at Lyosha who is already sitting down.

Inge? she says, and I go to the kitchen and carry in the big tureen filled with cold beet soup. As mother mutters grace over it, I peek at Alyosha, his mouth drawn down at the corners in his upside-down smile, his eyes like polished enamel, his irises neon green. Mother finishes; she and Kai cross themselves.

Is so very clean here, Lyosha says in his singsong German.

Thank you, says mother as she ladles the red soup into his dish.

I hope you did not have too much difficulty in finding the apartment?

No, I've been . . . no, not at all. Hmm, he continues, sniffing at the steam rising from his bowl. He takes his spoon and begins to slurp up the soup.

So delicious. Did you make it?

No, Inge did.

Such soup I have not had since I left Russia. I did not know such cooking was possible in Germany.

Mother starts asking him questions: where have you, how did you, how was, did you like. Lyosha answers briefly, but not too brusquely. The dinner limps from course to course this way, a yes, a no, a maybe, and our cuckoo clock ticking away the whole time. Then the clock chirps twice which makes Alyosha laugh, and his eyes move from it to the mahogany cupboard filled with little souvenirs, and he keeps on laughing as he takes in the Venetian glass, the postcards from Rumania and Yugoslavia, the brass windmill.

And how did you like New York? asks mother, and Alyosha launches into a series of funny stories about how he was chased by blacks everywhere. During the telling of the story, Alyosha pulls his face into a clown's mask, the full lips pulled down or smiling wide with his small rows of teeth—like milk teeth, but with a glint of silver showing here and there. His hair seems to crackle with life while Kai sits and smiles with his lips only.

My mother merely watches with her eyes slightly narrowed.

You like to travel, he says, tipping back his chair.

Yes, says mother, we used to. When my husband was still alive.

Why is it that Germans travel everywhere. Everywhere. I remember them in Moscow. Like a second invasion it was.

Was your father in the war? Kai asks.

No. He was too young. He spent it running from the Deutsch, I mean, from the Nazis. Never talked about it. The Nazis killed my grandfather for gathering firewood in the restricted area. He had lousy timing. If he'd just stayed in the Gulag, he might've made it, but they released him, and boom.

Wars are so awful, say mother. In Poland had two invasions.

Only two?

Two are enough. First the Germans, who were not so very bad. They put an officer in our house, but he was very polite and well bred, and even shared his rations with us. Otherwise, we may have starved. Then came the Russians. We heard stories. Urinated against the few walls left standing. Then the Ukrainians. They ripped the faucets from the kitchen and the toilet, and then stuck them in another wall.

Why?

They had never seen plumbing before. They thought that they could stick a pipe into any wall and have water come out.

Ukrainians are pigs. It's true.

He twists around in his chair to look out the window that gives on to the courtyard of our apartment. The clock ticks away.

Pulling a cigarette from his pack, Alyosha says, nice courtyard.

I start to giggle.

Tell me, says my mother, what will you do when you stop dancing?

I won't.

Won't what? Stop dancing?

Yes.

You mean, mother says, that you will become a choreographer? A teacher? There are several ballet teachers here in Cologne. You remember Frau Borman, Inge? She does good business training dancers. In fact, she just moved into a new studio in a very nice neighborhood.

I do not intend to teach.

But what will you do? A dancer's career, as I understand it, is quite limited.

Just dance, he says, wiping his mouth with his napkin, and tossing it on to the table, that's all.

But you have only a few years left as a dancer.

We shall see.

Even famous dancers. . . her voice trails off and she smiles a tight, apologetic smile.

I am still young. I am still capable. I will dance until I decide to stop dancing. What do you know about it, anyway? Have you seen me dance? Do you know even the slightest, tiniest bit about dancing? No, of course you don't. You don't know anything, do you? So why are you insulting me? Should I insult you back? Tell you that your are a stinking old sow? That you. . .

He chokes.

Mother sits and does nothing, her face paralyzed into a mask of itself. I can't breathe. I can't move. I've never seen anything like this at my table. And for a crazy second, I'm glad that he did what I never dared to,

Get out, Kai shouts. Get out and never come here again, and Kai breaks the spell. He grabs Alyosha by the shirt and yanks him from the chair. Alyosha pushes him away.

I'm going, don't worry about that, you fucking pitiful slob. Just get your shitty hands off of me. Thank you so much for dinner, Inge.

The door slams. My mother weeps silently, shaking her head from side to side.

Lyosha

Ended by leaving Cologne with the company. Had to. Nothing else to do. Otherwise, I lose a job. Then have every other company director ask, Why did you leave the company in mid season?

For love, Mr. Director sir, for love.

Real dancers love only dancing and themselves. Next, please.

Was sorry to leave her. But, nothing else I could do except make promises, yes, I'll write, I'll be back at the end of the season please please wait for me. Maybe I'm not a passionate man, maybe not, but I know. Still. Only a girl, who waited back stage like the other girls in the other towns.

Would follow me, she said, would write to me. Never did. Thought some Manfred locked her up in Valhalla, put a horned helmet on her head so they could eat potatoes, sausage and sauerkraut together and sing Wagner arias to the thump of beer steins on a table.

Two months passed like that with her in the back of my skull, or under my skin. Like a big hook your belly. Then slowly you begin to love the pain of being away as much as you love the blonde ghost who drifts beside you, floating under your eyelids above those paisley patterns as you fall to sleep, a permanent fixture of your life like the never ending series of hotel room and as intimate as the stale smell of cigarettes that clings to your clothes. Wrote to her. Postmarked Bonn, Hanover, Strasbourg, Hamburg, Frieburg, Krautburg et cetera et cetera until finally Stuttgart, the last town on the tour.

After Stuttgart, back on the streets again, auditioning for the next season with this company or another company and start kissing ass. Oh, and standing in line with the entire emigrant population of the third world to see if some round-faced paper pusher will give you your unemployment, waiting for letters from Mamasha with money. Too little, too late.

So Stuttgart. Five performances. After Sunday, it was all over. Just the train back to Rotterdam and try to squeeze out your oh so tearful farewells to the boys and girls, the girls and the girls and the boys and the boys.

Such bullshit in the ballet. You hate this boy: then suddenly you share little tears at farewell time, a big show, please write, we'll stay in touch, you know where you'll be? Ah, with *that* company, a knowing nod, good luck. Okay, he may be an asshole. True. Still, the company doesn't pay badly, so I'll shed a few tears just in case I get a place there next season. But, this is what they're all thinking under the theatrics: make it forever, this oh so painful separation. Don't come back and audition for *my* place, because I don't need you or your competition, I've got problems of my own, so just stay good and fucked off.

Finally comes the last performance of those shitty ballets with their utterly pedestrian choreography, and thank God for that. Stage lights out, costumes turned in.

Stayed on another day at the hotel, gratis thanks to the proprietor who hoped to get his hands on one of the girls. The last, double paycheck nestles in my pocket with the forms for the government dole filled out by the business manager.

In a Stuttgart beer garden. Surrounded by American soldiers in crew cuts and earrings—the earrings to camouflage the fact that they are soldiers. Instead, they look like escapees from a leather bar.

Glass of vodka in front of me, served by a cow in a red checked dirndl, her boobs jiggling about the low cut bodice. Nice show. The red checkered tablecloth matched her dress: orderly touch. Things

24

match in Deutschland. Plastic ivy wound up the white trellis facing me. In such a scene—such a miserable scene—what would be wrong with a little self pity? A tiny bit of misogyny, too, when those creatures think that because they take you in between their legs that they become queens over you, rule you, torture you with their little tricks and smiles.

And all the time it is you who should forget them. Like Baryshnikov and his little cherries that he picks, one by one. See if you could catch that little monster, Misha B., sitting around in a cheap deutscher bar thinking about some slut of a girl who gives herself away on the second night an thinks so little of it that she can't spare the two minutes it would take to write two lines, if only to say, you're miserable and worthless, so leave me alone.

Guten abend, intoned a fruity voice carried on waves of eau de cologne. Turned to see an old man. With silver hair combed straight back from a high brow only slightly creased with wrinkles. Could have been von Karajan's twin. Who was offering me a drink.

Noch ein vodka, bitte.

After having secured permission, he alights on the chair across the table, waving for the waitress, the light glinting on the rings on his fingers.

Who said he recognized me from the ballet the night before (ah, the joys of fame!) and found my dancing to be truly excellent, as good as the lead's.

Had to admire not only the clearness of his sight, but also the quality of his taste—in dancing, if not in dress. Wide lapels on his blue velveteen sports coat, with an ascot. To hide the wattles, no doubt.

Lighting my cigarette with a wafer-thin silver lighter, he offered champagne for the next round. On him. Which I accepted.

Such an interesting accent I had. So well the Deutsch I spoke. Had to ask him, in return, for his biography. Had composed in his youth, but regrettably was without talent. Took a law degree and went into the family business. His teeth gleamed in porcelain rows—were they real?

Luckily, he admitted sotto voce, he had a modest talent for commerce. Excuses himself for a trip to the W.C., holding his stomach in on the way. Didn't want to display his tummy. How thoughtful. Considered leaving, but the bottle of champagne was there.

Marriage, divorce, long thoughtful pulls of the cigarette. Would you like some saucisson lyonnaise?

Still regretted that he had given up the piano, so tried to make up for it with outings to the, unfortunately rather mediocre, companies in town, but. Another bottle?

Why not?

Spare the rest of the details, except for the way the table began to sway gently from side to side. Finished by offering me a ride to my hotel. Taxis, he said, were rather dear in Stuttgart, and it wouldn't trouble him at all. Out the door and across the asphalt, the soldiers slamming each other on the back behind us.

Opened the door of the Mercedes for me. Which smelled of leather and his cologne.

Perhaps, before I returned to my hotel, I would take a drink at his apartment? It isn't far from here.

Accepted.

Purrs over the cobblestones, the asphalt, shadows streaking through the windows followed by street lamps light.

Continued his patter as his hand wafted down delicately like a nauseated butterfly on my thigh.

27

Swung into a courtyard, then whisked up in an elevator to the top floor. His floor.

Woke the in the still-dark morning with bile burning the back of my throat and a raging need to piss. Next to an old man, who, when he snored, breathed out the stench of slowly rotting meat. Who groaned but did not wake when I slipped out of the stained satin sheets and picked up my jeans and shirt from the Persian rug.

Noticed, as I picked up a sock, the cashmere jacket hung on the back of a chair. From the pockets of which he had drawn a lambskin wallet the night before. Glanced at the lump in bed. Which still snored.

Reached into that pocket, still watching him. To find the wallet, draw out the bills and slip them in my shoes. Left the door of the bedroom open behind me and crept down the—thank God! --- thickly carpeted stairs into his living room with my heart thumping, expecting some witch of a housemaid to catch me and beat me with a broom. Turned the brass doorknob with a wet palm, then out into the hall, down the rest of the stairs, trying not to run. Into the courtyard, out the gate and on the main street. Lived in the center of town, he did; more good luck.

Took a leak away from the light of the street lamps, just beginning to fade with the approaching morning. In the tired linden tree, a bird sang louder than my heart.

My god, you're hung like a horse.

Turned. A girl, no, a hooker leaned against the lamp post. Chubby and nearly too young.

Fuck off.

Laughter. Then, come on, you can put that thing to better use. Come with me.

No. I'm all fucked out, I said and zipped my pants.

Come with me cutie, she said, as she tottered towards me on stiletto heels.

You're too sexy to be out by yourself. Hand on my crotch, thick smell of perfume and cigarettes wafting up. Turkish, with thick black hair a white smile, the whites of her eyes glowing. Took my hand, then wrapped her arm around my waist.

You're so sexy, so sexy with such nice muscles she kept whispering and drew me to a narrow alley, steering me by my waist, occasionally rubbing the cheeks of my tired ass.

Stop. I told you, I'm tired.

Don't worry. I'll take good care of you.

Smiled even wider, but in her eyes, fear, worry, the shadow of some pimp who'd beat the hell out of her if she didn't bring back enough marks to whatever lamb-reeking, garlic-stinking shit hole she lived in.

Turned and shook her ass at me.

You don't like? You take me however you like? Rubbed her breasts, then shimmied her belly against mine, moving up and down. Moustache above the wide red mouth.

See? You like me. It shows.

Pulled me into a corridor with yellow walls and fluorescent lights, unlocked a door and we went down a hall smelling of herring and intimate dirt. Public housing. Kept steering me, stroking me giggling, frantic. Hid her eyes from me. Afraid I'd escape, when she wasn't bad, not really my style, an under-aged whore, not really my taste.

Hastily fumbled with keys from her tiny white purse. Through a red door and into a room, a closet, with nothing but a bed, a potted palm, a few mirrors, a piece of crap ebony faux Cameroon nude sculpture, some porno posters on the wall. Unbuttons my pants and pulls them down so I can negotiate in the nude. Unzips her black vinyl bustier and puts my hand on the small mound of her breast. Names a price for full treatment.

Slipped off my shoe and passed over the wad of bank notes, easily five times as much as she asked for and as a bonus, delicately smelling of expensive cologne as well as my dirty sock. She starts gasping and crying—new to the job, and so still capable of sincere feelings—and overwhelmed, crawls onto me, sobbing.

What can I say? Must have been my worthless goddam socialist training, transferring money like that from rich fag to poor whore. Robin fucking Hood. Hated myself already for doing it.

Tells me she's willing to do anything, anything, anything.

Left right away, or I might have tried.

Quick march to the hotel, rubbing the grit out of my eyes and saw the predawn fog like sour milk pouring itself over the very tidy streets, past the trucks delivering beer to the bars. With my bag, hurried to the train station, the beginnings of a headache prying its way between the tip of my spine and the base of my head, the champagne boiling up in acid bubbles.

Tickets to Cologne? Too much money, in my present financial circumstances. Have to save.

Inge

Inge! Kai shouts from the vestibule into the kitchen. Martin's on the phone.

I put down the dishrag.

I can say you're not at home.

No, I'll come.

I dry my hands on the blue towel and walk to the entryway where Kai hands me the receiver, shrugging his shoulders, as if he doesn't want to be blamed for whatever will happen.

Inge? Martin says

Please don't hang up. Can we talk?

I turn to face the corner, wishing my mother would let me smoke inside the apartment.

I asked you not to call me. I don't have anything to say to you.

Wait. Can you listen to me? Just listen for a minute. You owe that much to me after everything.

I can almost see him flick his shoeblack hair out of his eyes and lean his face into mine while he looks at his feet.

What do you want, Martin?

Listen.

I'm listening.

No, listen to me: We should have stayed together, you and me.

Next to the telephone a crystal vase stands, filled with a bouquet of white roses that my mother's boyfriend gave to her. The roses are beginning□□ to wilt, going brown around the edges of the petals, almost as if they had been bruised.

Why are you calling me now—after five months? Why do you have to do these things to me? It's over. Are . . . are you high or something?

No fucking way. I'm off the hard shit. That's why I, I mean, maybe since I . . .Since I'm clean, you know?

My cat, Salome, starts rubbing against my leg, purring, then jumps on the chair beside the stand.

And what about what you said to me? Those horrible things? And you tried to. You tried to. . . when you were going to . . .

He interrupts: It was just craziness. And the drugs, the space I was in. That's all. I'm sorry. I've said I'm sorry a million million times. I love you Inge. You know I'm not like that.

No, I don't know. That's why I don't want to have anything to do with you.

Oh, Inge, he groans. I miss you so fucking bad. I just want to see you. I don't care about the other guy.

What other guy? What guy?

That skinny guy with the short hair. The foreigner. Andreas said you were hanging out with him. But I don't care.

That's good. Because I don't care about you—or Johanna either.

I never would have seen her if you hadn't left me. I was just messed up.

She's a slut. How could you go with her?

So what? I just wanted to piss you off, that's all.

It doesn't matter. I don't care who you see, who you're with, what you care about, what you don't care about.

Salome climbs on the table and starts gnawing on the ferns on the edge of the vase.

Then, he whispers in his strangled voice, why are you talking to me. I know you care. I love you Inge.

Traffic rushes in the background.

I really do. So fucking bad, so bad. That's why I . . .that's why things get so crazy. But if it's too much for you to be with me again, be my lover, then it's cool—we could just see each other. Friends.

We'll never be friends.

Remember? he asks, remember how great it used to be? Just being together. Going dancing, or hanging out by ourselves. Maybe watching some television. We had a lot. Remember when you could come over and spend the night? Doesn't that mean anything to you?

That was a long time ago.

We can't just fuck it all up now, because of a fight.

I push Salome away from the flowers; she lands on the floor.

Sorry, I say to Salome, but in the receiver, so Martin says, It's cool. All I want is to see you. Just once. Then we'll know for sure. And if you don't like me, if you don't feel anything, then, okay, it's over. Settled.

What about Johanna?

It's over. You call her now and you ask her if you don't believe me. She'll tell you.

And you quit the hard stuff?

Just smoke a joint now and then, y'know, a little hash is all. I went through the program at the Herman Hesse Center.

He pauses. I did it for you.

You should have done it for yourself.

Look, just for an hour, any place you want to meet. If I make you puke, okay, walk away and we won't see each other again. But I have to see you. One more time.

For an hour?

Ten minutes. Whatever. On Friday?

Friday?

At the Ring Café. If you want.

I'll bring Petra with me.

No problem. It's totally up to you.

Okay, four o'clock.

Thanks, Inge. You're like a fucking saint.

Lyosha

Come with me to Paris, I said.

Lyosha, you know I can't.

Arrived in Cologne. Enough money for a few months, with the paycheck, maybe some unemployment too, and then another job. Mother in

36

Paris too, she would help us. To live together, make a new life. Wished I had five times, ten times, a thousand times the money, to shower on her, bury her in it and take her away with me, to live together forever.

Why promise me at all, then, why even say that you love me if you don't mean it. You lied to me.

It wasn't a lie, Lyosha.

Then come with me. What's stopping you?

My mother . . .

Your mother. Your mother. You're not a baby. You're grown up. Forget your mother. You complained and complained about her, and now, when you can . . .

I'm only nineteen. I need to do my course at the Institute.

Nineteen is already too old. You get older and older then you die and rot, if you're lucky. What's your age got to do with it? Paris is beautiful. Beautiful. You told me you're bored. You said you wanted to travel. That you wanted to see Paris finally. So come with me.

No, she said. I'm sorry, but no.

What?

Okay, so you have a boyfriend. Someone you didn't tell me about, some skinhead storm trooper. Some idiot. I'll give you everything. Everything. And what can he do that I can't?

Looked over the park. Elm leaves turning yellow, and the fallen leaves stirring on the cobblestone paths. Green bench we sat on seemed to rock like a boat caught in a wave, the mud between my shoes rising and falling. Treated like a buffoon on a drunken boat. Turned her back to me, so all I could see was the hair falling past her shoulder and the curve of her side. To know I had had that same soft swell in my hand, but now.

You're humiliating me.

Not so loud, they can hear us.

I don't care. Do you love him?

Lyosha, I. . .

There, you see? You don't love him. If you did, you would say so. And you cannot.

How can I leave?

Pack your fucking bag. Say goodbye. The train leaves every day. Anything else you need, I can give you.

Turning to face forward, she fumbled in her small black purse for a cigarette and tried to light it, but the wind kept blowing out the flame. Her small hard mouth, drawn tight, shrouded by the blonde hair which kept blowing in her face and sticking to her cheeks. Wet with tears. Brushed her hair away from her face and said, Who are you to come and bother me? What right do you have to come between my mother and me? Between my boyfriend and me? How can you push me with nothing but promises. You are the one who is lying. You.

I'm not forcing. You said that you loved me. I love you. So come.

I love my family too. I have a good job. What will happen when we get there? What would I do in Paris? I can't even speak French.

What does it matter what you do?

You're so. . . so . . . emotional. We had an affair. We spent some time together. Just an affair. Now you want to kidnap me.

So that's it? Nothing we did means anything to you. Fun. It was fun. Very fun.

No, but. . .

And you can lie so easily. With your eyes, with your mouth. With your body. You just lied to me. Now it's sorry. Good bye, asshole. Loser.

Oh God.

Followed her gaze to a group of boys passing around a bottle under the bandstand roof.

I have to go now, she said.

Wait. Wait, I pulled her arm. Here is my address in Paris. Gave her the card my mother had sent me.

Stared at me full in the face, for the first time. Those blue rises surrounded by red veins. The mascara on her face: black ruts smudging her cheeks:

If you love me, how can you be so cruel?

I tell you what is cruel. To say you love someone when you don't. Now that—that is fucking cruel.

I'm going.

Released her arm.

You say I make promises. You say I lied to you. Here they are, my lies and my promises. Took all the bills in my pocket, all those pretty pieces of German paper, and threw them in her lap, at that pink face, half-wishing, no, wanting them to be coins so they could hit that swollen sloppy mess and hurt her as much as she was hurting me. So I got up and walked away before she could see me give way.

Looked back. Couldn't help myself.

Turned back. And saw her picking up the wind-scattered notes.

Inge

The radiator clicks on, then hisses heat into our living room. A north wind rattles the shutters behind the closed curtains. Mama sets her glasses down on the open page of her Sunday magazine, and, clearing her throat, asks Kai.

When did you let Salome out?

Around dinnertime, he says, returning to his book.

I can't imagine what she's doing out on a night like this. She rises, takes a few steps to the window, then hesitates.

I'm sure she'll be back any minute. I told the caretaker to watch for her. She probably has a romance with some nice tomcat.

We have too many romances in this family. We should fix her before she has another litter.

Mama runs her hand along the curtain, then says as she glances at the cuckoo clock. It's past 10:30 already. I'm going to bed. I have to get up early tomorrow. Monday again.

41

She trudges to the hall door, slides it open. Please remember to turn off the lights before you go to sleep. And Kai?

Yes?

If Salome comes back, please wake me.

Before she passes through the door, she reminds us not to stay up late. We say our good nights. She slides the door shut. The water gurgles in the radiator pipes, and a toilet flushes. Someone clumps down the hall outside.

It's cold tonight, I say.

Very, Kai nods.

Do you think Salome's all right?

Sure.

What are you reading?

Without looking up he says, *The Blue Angel.*

How is it?

Yes it is. Very good.

It is the sort of an autumn night when you are alone, whether or not you are with people, and it seems that you will stay alone for the rest of your life, washed in loneliness like an empty bench in the park under the rain. The whole world shrinks into a dark corner, but no one understands that. Even if you could ring someone on the telephone, they would sound bored with you and your stories. Nothing is on the television, the cooking is finished, and you have a read all the books that day that you possibly could. Outside of the apartment on a night like that, it always rains or drizzles, and the sky sinks down in heavy clouds which smother you like sodden wool.

The door buzzer screeches. I jump. Kai runs to the intercom to ask who's there.

Only static spits through the speaker.

Some one's playing a prank, Kai says.

Maybe someone's found Salome. Shouldn't we go downstairs and see?

Kai picks up the keys from the telephone table, hands me my coat and then we wait for the elevator in the hall. Kai opens the frosted glass doors for me; the elevator sinks to the ground floor. Herr Gefunden is kneeling by the entryway, his white shirted back framed in the doorway. He clambers up, and peering over the tops of his glasses shouts,

Who's there?

Kai and Inge Hasen, number 669.

The family with the black cat?

Yes.

You'd better come here, he says to Kai. You, he says to me, stay inside . . .Out of the wind.

I try to follow, but Herr Gefunden makes a sign to Kai, and Kai asks me please won't you stay in the lobby. Please.

He follows Herr Gefunden out of the vestibule. Through my reflection in the glass panes of the doors, I can see them talking, the shadows from the porch light finding their way in to the hollows of the faces. Kai glances at me, then turns away. Their faces disappear, then reappear in the glass, Kai nodding his head rapidly. Herr Gefunden unlocks the door and opens it for Kai.

What's going on?

The manager slips down the hall on the left.

Is it Salome?

Kai stands next to me, looking at his shoes which left little rust-colored prints on the tiled floor, then he takes my arm.

Inge . . . Salome. He releases my arm, fumbles with his keys.

Oh.

The center of me drains slowly out, leaving nothing but a gaping hole.

He found Salome. Someone cut her throat and dumped her. Herr Gefunden saw them—a bunch of guys in leather jackets. They were spray painting something on the door when he saw them, and he chased them away. Inge? I'll take care of Salome.

At the end of the hollowness, a sea of acid surges up through the vacuum, strangling my throat before it springs out of my two blind eyes.

Lyosha

Asked for my key, and the concierge handed it to me. With a blue envelope. With Inge's name in the upper right-hand corner. Put it in my bag with the bread, sausage and white wine I'd bought for dinner. Went up the seven flights of spiraling stairs to my room. Unlocked the door and placed it, the envelope, that envelope with the rest of my groceries on the red bedspread.

Waited only a month to write. Wanted first to burn that sky-blue envelope on the bed, flush it down the bidet in the corner, but remembered that bidets don't flush.

How could she have sent a letter? Now. To me. What could she possibly have to say after that little scene in the park? Bent down to pick it up, bumping my head against the sloping ceiling, then sliced the crisp envelope open with my knife and sat on the bed in the light from the window to read it.

> Dear Alyosha (*nice start*),
>
> Now I realize that you're right (*only now?*) Please, if you can, let me come to you and love you *(Why not? Why should a little greed, a little betrayal stand in the way?*). Your face, your mouth, your voice have haunted me for the last month, and will haunt me forever. I will make you happier than anyone in the world, because you brought me that happiness when we were together. Please forgive me for being so stupid. Please tell me when to come, and I will come, wherever, whenever. I will wait for your word forever, and I will always love you, no matter what. I'm so sorry, but I believe that love can win over everything, even a mistake like mine. I ache for you Alyosha,
>
> Love,
>
> Inge.
>
> PS I still have the money.

Crumpled it up. Tore it up. Threw it in the wastepaper basket, then kicked that stinking can. Pieces of the letter fluttered onto the brown carpet, along with the cigarette butts, the orange peels and the empty milk bottle. Stepped over the mess to open the window, which gave out on to a courtyard.

Caught a girl undressing across from me. Who saw me and threw the curtains together. Two pigeons were cooing, perched on the eaves above my head. Maybe, I thought, a sign from Cupid.

Then something white splattered on the sill next to my hand.

Grabbed my coat, went back to the stairs, deposited the keys with the mustachioed but arguably female concierge and pushed my way out on to the street, letting the crowd on Boulevard Clichy pick me up in its stream.

Chose a bench on the island dividing the two streams of traffic, a spot away from the group of clochards huddled together, and wiped away the chestnut leaves which had turned the color of dried tobacco. To stare at the crowd opposite me, filing past the narrow shops lighted with livid white, the better to show off the cheap bolts of cloth or the stereos.

So what. Split myself open for her, turned myself inside out so that I was nothing but the lining of my mouth, and she raked her claws across that. Me.

She, who wanted to stay with her mama, her boyfriend, her cabbage life. What she wanted, then.

And now: the unbelievable, the incredible nerve, and the sorry little vulgarity of running after that money, those bills. Chased them and ignored me. Showing all her scarlet neon whore colors. Diseased. A sick person, poisoned and cold. Then, to write, Queen to slave, Field Marshal to private.

Must have been talking aloud. A grande dame in a fake fur walking her poodle made a wide circle around me, her dog straining the leash to have a smell of the leg of the bench for the neighborhood news. My bulletins come in lying words.

Words. Words in purple ink. Letters so neatly formed in purple ink. So legible. Such proper schoolgirl style. The hands that held that pen. The same small hands with the bitten nails, those hands had been on my lips, on my back, on my ass. Pulled off a shirt, unhooked a bra and unbuttoned her jeans so she could stand still in the moonlight. To offer all she had: the smiling shadow of her belly, the twin curving breasts, mouth, and hand.

Her mind, though. But then who cares? If once, just once, she stood like that, offering herself, free and sheeted in silver. Rest of it was just her mother's training, the dry voice counting pfennigs in the background.

Stood up. Shaft of a street led up the hill, revealing the tit of Sacré Coeur.

Who can make you feel. That you have feelings, even if it is hate wrapped in acid and thrown at a face. Had the how, the why, then didn't matter. Loved me enough to come crawling back, even if in just a letter. Okay, let's say bored. Maybe only bored she was. If she could offer that much, I'd do the rest.

Inge

I arrive in Gare de l'Est, the electronic voices of announcers echoing through the station. On the platform some Americans knock into me with their huge backpacks. Gray light filters through the skylights overhead, water-like, catching the sun bleached hair of the Americans or glistening on the dark hair of short, nervous men in suits who are hopping like pigeons to get through the lines of the passengers. I can't see him anywhere down the length of the platform or among the luggage carts and the blue-suited conductors. And old man comes rushing out of the stream of people and embraces the woman next to me and their faces dissolve in tears mixed with kisses.

I walk the length of the train, worried now by the absence of Lyosha, trying to see past the bobbing heads, wondering how he could be late, or if, perhaps, he isn't here at all. Black Africans with big teeth, the pale light shining blue on their skins, are drinking in a stand-up bar. Arabs seem to be everywhere, smoking as they lean against the fat pillars. One, in a blue-striped jacket with his shirt unbuttoned, wearing read jeans streaked with grease, one stares at me.

Someone takes my arm; I turn and it's Lyosha, smiling as he leans over to kiss me. I pull away slightly, but he holds me even harder and kisses me more deeply. He releases me to ask questions that anyone asks at the end of a train trip. He takes my bag and leads me down the broad stairs to the Metro below, faces flowing upward carried by the escalator as we descend. A urine smell mixed with the smoke from the French cigarettes flows around us.

When we reach the lower level, Lyosha walks over to the Metro plan on the wall. Rows of lockers line the wall; more people passing, checking their watches, dragging on cigarettes, the high heels of the women's shoes clicking on the floor. From where I stand, the map of Paris looks like a plan for a multi-colored spider's web. An old man in a black suit and tie comes up to me and asks something in French, and seeing my blank look, switches to English to ask me if I am lost. He smiles and shows a row of sulfur-yellow teeth.

No, I say.

No, Lyosha shouts, we are not lost. The man turns, still smiling and melts into the line of people climbing the stairs.

Who was he? Lyosha asks.

I don't know.

Money is safe?

Yes. He didn't come near me.

Good. So you are ready to go Montmartre?

Can't we rest for a minute?

Okay. He folds his arms across his chest, lowering his head to glower at the passers by. Lyosha says, You will like it much better once we are out of here and above the ground.

Why does it stink like a rotten egg?

He shrugs.

Don't know. Lucky it doesn't smell of something worse. Maybe it's the blacks. He turns to me with a sigh. Are you ready or not?

51

Yes. Is it very far from here?

No problem. We'll be there soon.

He takes my suitcase and we walk down a long hallway paved with gray tiles. I feel as if I'm inside an eel. We descend still deeper on more escalators. When we reach the turnstile, Lyosha looks at the booth where a uniformed man and a woman are talking to each other, and he vaults over the metal bar. An old woman looks at him and shakes her head as he passes.

Lyosha, you have to pay.

Hand me the bags.

We have to pay . . . What happens if we get caught?

Don't argue. Hand me the bag.

Lyosha please . . .

Listen to me: We're not in Deutschland anymore. No one cares about these stupid rules here.

But they'll catch us.

No, they won't. Just hand me the damn bag and get over here.

I pass the bags over the turnstile, and after glancing at the glass booth where the two controllers are still talking to each other, I slip under the bar, smudging the knees of my pants.

Was that so hard?

No. I just don't like to do those things. It's not honest.

We descend another fight of stairs past a one-eyed man in a filthy blue coat who is holding out his hand palm up. At the toes of his cracked boots is a cardboard sign with merci scrawled on it.

As we wait for the train, the air weighs on me, something you can touch and spread over your body like tar. A stale sigh of wind comes from the two dark holes at either end of the tunnel. On the wall across the tracks are a line of huge posters: a picture of Adam and Eve with her breasts showing, an advertisement for a language school, a picture of a bald man with his head lined in orange and his mouth open—for a film called *Journal d'un fou*; and another for an opera, *Salome*. Salome. Four bums beneath the posters pass a bottle of wine and argue in phlegm-coated voices.

Train's coming, says Lyosha, and we move to the edge of the platform. For a minute I'm afraid of falling onto the rails. The train arrives with a squeal of metal on metal, a series of plate glass windows, breaking and scattering the light into fragments of faces and bits of glare, the doors which open and

53

vomit a stream of passengers and we fight our way through the departing riders, taking our seats as the doors shut behind us. The subway cars jolt us into the darkness at the edge of the platform.

Lyosha

Woke late, the triangle of the sky showing itself sapphire bright above the mottled grey wall. Inge dreaming beside me. Wrapped in the sheets. Smelling of sleep. Vanilla. Old apples.

Stepped out the door and closed it softly behind me. Down the stairs, across the courtyard, passing the grey garbage pails with their orange lids and out to the street. Held my jacket to my throat to close in the warmth against the wind which whipped my breath out of me. Turned left to the baker's where a flour-pale fat blonde handed breakfast baguettes to women in long coats. Stood in line.

Trois croissants de beurre, s'il vous plait.

Paused before she reached behind the glass case. Blue eyes glared down the long bumpy line of her nose.

Au beurre, she corrected.

Au beurre, au beurre, au beurre. Trois.

Handed the croissants wrapped up, with pudgy fingers. After counting the change carefully.

Took the six flights of stairs two at a time. Entered, paused. Room swims in purple after the sunlight. Bed surfaced out of the shadows. And on the bed, a tangled of sunshine-colored hair at the pillow. Her hand, baby-like, curled next to her sighing mouth opened against the sheets. Red lips. Which I kissed. To waken the woman, who stretched out in the bed and rose, letting the blanket fall, her nipples puckering in the chill. Two more kisses, on the breasts still holding the womb warmth of the bed. Which I melted into after tearing off shoes, shirt and trousers, forgetting my cold feet in the tangle of hot and cold limbs, her pearl soft skin below me and the coarse blanket on my back, losing my tongue in the sweet and sour mouth which turned into a summer strawberry.

Afterwards, the room resolved itself into chipped corners. Stained sheets. Spotted ceiling. And three croissants.

Hungry?

Starved.

Served the croissants with the orange juice taken in from the windowsill. Pastry flakes clung to a smiling lip wanting to be kissed again. Even after having been bruised to the color of fall roses.

Inge

When you find someone you love, the world is like the inside of a shell. When he takes you by the hand and he walks with you along the banks of a river which slows slowly under the old bridges and away into the big dark sea. Or you walk together by cafés smelling of coffee and burned sugar and solitary old women in blue raincoats smile at you and you feel the pressure of his hand in yours. A stone bench becomes dear to you one day in the Jardin du Luxembourg as you look at little children sailing boats in a fountain in front of a palace built by a queen and you wonder if, maybe one day our children will. When you are in love, you discover how two bodies can fit perfectly together, whether he holds you on a corner of a street, at a table in a restaurant, or in a narrow bed.

Lyosha

Resumed classes with Mme. Razumskaya. A lady of the Old School. Who danced at the Bolshoi when she was still a young thing, before her skin crinkled and turned elephant grey from chain smoking. Said to have escaped Comrade Joe's notice by sleeping first with the NKVD then with a Westerner who spirited her away from Odessa with a fake passport. Was said to have been a nymphomaniac, not that you can tell now, what with her body curled over on itself. Bone disease. Put an end to her career, but not as a teacher. Banging and screeching from the corner of the overheated studio. Scowling under heavy brows with red-rimmed eyes, eyes that pick out the least, the smallest, near infinitesimal mistake.

Who's asking, but it's a terrible thing to be a dancer. Horrible. Three days away from the barre and your legs and back begin to stiffen. Like a corpse already. Only gets worse when you're twenty-eight. Twenty-eight! The leg doesn't hold the posit ion without a little tremor, the thighs betray you during a jetté that two years ago you could execute without a thought. Tendons know, and the belly. The belly pouches out even at the thought of a pastry.

Classes. In the same studio with the same wooden floor, a barre running along a mirror, some windows to let in ashen city light. A battered upright piano. A teacher, transformed by age into a sadistic maniac, who was always better than you will ever be. Who demands a level of perfection still unseen by human eyes. Who tortures you for the youth that you have and that was robbed from her at the peak of her skill. Outside the studio, she's nothing. They're all nothing, the teachers, those creaky-voiced dying swans. Nothing. Little people with too many scarves who get pushed around by thick-wristed oafs.

But inside: Napoleons. Caesars. Gods. If you don't like it—boom, out on your ass. Because three hundred other pieces of meat in toe shoes are panting away, ready to jump in your spot.

Biography of a dancer: Mama takes you to your first class. Lets go of your hand. You leave with your toe shoes a few years later. Mount the stairs, and you exit in New York, dripping sweat, your work out clothes stinking up the subway. Same studio in Toronto—the same damn room. Bend over the barre, and you step out to buy a sandwich in Rotterdam.

Leave the studio again, and you find yourself in a narrow Parisian hallway sneaking a cigarette. Theatres, applause, dressing rooms, busses, girlfriends, boy friends, they're just what happens in between classes.

Masochist and idiot that I am, I sign up for two full classes a day. Seven hours. But I don't have a choice, really. Have to do it, endure that bitch's gimlet eyes, the searing lungs, the twitching muscles, the aching knees. Because, yes ladies and gentlemen, because I love the dance.

Inge

Sometimes when I lie on the bed with Lyosha sleeping beside me, I listen to him breathe, then I time my breaths so we inhale and exhale in the same rhythm. Imagining the while that our souls seep out of our mouths, mingling together in the way our breaths blend. In the darkness of the room, I see our spirits floating above us, shimmering, hovering; his glows red while mine is purple. They merge, all purity, away from this clay, these lumps we have to drag around with us all day. Our souls, when we were first together, were distinct, but now the limbs, the arms and legs melt and all that is left above us is a ball,

59

rolled up into one being, hanging in the stillness of our room.

If I fall asleep after they merge, I feel it above us all night as I sleep and dream. They warm the room. But, if Lyosha groans, or shifts in his sleep, he breaks the spell, the ball disappears, and I cannot sleep for a long time after that because it is a sign that we shall argue the next day. Or I raise myself on my elbow and study Lyosha's face, to see why our souls cannot grow together. If he is frowning, it means he has a nightmare. Or, if his face is calm, boyish, I do not mind so much because I can study him as he was in the past.

But other nights, no matter how hard I try, I can neither see our souls nor make them blend. Then I weep, listening to the sound of the cars and the heels pounding on the pavement outside our windows. It is then that demons are around, and it is they who are breaking the spell.

Lyosha

Turned left from the Rue de Rennes to Boulevard Montparnasse. Squeezed through the crowd held back by pastry stalls and kiosks. Gained the wide sidewalk, noticed that the plane trees were budding. Took Inge's hand and proposed a drink at the Rotonde.

Why that café?

Because it is home to famous painters, writers and dancers. Nijinsky used to eat caviar there. And besides, I don't have to see that goddamn Tour Montparnasse.

Seated at a table. Followed statue Balzac's scowl across the crowded boulevard to the Dome. March wind fluttered the suit coats and skirts of the passers by. Behind the plate glass at my back, the scent of well-groomed money, faces smoothed and perfumed, lit discreetly at the tables. Inge's sun-warmed hair brushed across my cheek.

But isn't it too expensive for us?

What's the use of being in Paris if you can't treat yourself? To just a coffee.

But I don't see the difference between this or any other café.

But it is where Sartre, that idiot, was. This is where Picasso was. Diaghelev. Trotsky.

You're just chasing ghosts.

I like my ghosts.

Drew back. To dig in her purse for cigarettes papers and tobacco.

I don't see anyone like that here now, she said. Just some rich wives and some businessmen out for a late lunch.

They're just distractions.

And so the bill will be too—a distraction.

The wind kept blowing the tobacco from the paper. Giving up, she rolled the unused paper into a ball and put them in the ashtray.

Pouting, she turned her face away from me. A tiny ear, coral-colored, I kissed. She smiled at me.

A favor.

Maybe after you get a job we can go to these places. But it's silly to pay as much for two coffees as we would for a whole dinner.

Of course, she was right. Understood, even as I said, you have such good sense. Such good sense, all the time. How does it feel to be so sensible? Or does it take any feelings at all to be a little cash register, counting all the pfennigs?

I'm only trying to help us. How can we stay together if we run completely out of money? How can we?

Her voice teetered on the edge of tears.

Be reasonable, Lyosha. It's been a month since we've had any new money at all, and the rent will be due. You know how it is with us. So why waste money to sit with these pretentious jerks? You're the one who says he hates bourgeois assholes, so why do you want to sit with them?

Left the café. Without even having our order taken.

Inge

I'm so sore there . . . down there, between my legs, sore from so much love, more sex than even Martin wanted, that is what he takes from me. From love making so much I feel completely swollen and heavy.

My skin becomes new and raw and doubly sensitive, so when he starts again, it hurts almost, it is right on the border of pain as he takes my nipples in his mouth once again, or as he lightly bites my throat. But I myself can become all passionate again, and the pain is replaced by warmth, by heat and hunger so I press his head against my belly, or my breast, or I draw his lips to mine to taste his tongue. A sort of madness comes over me, and I want to draw all of him into me, finger, tongue, all of him at once. Other times, I want to have him, I wish to penetrate, to sink deep into his body, to posses him the way the takes me, and I press hard against him, against his slender hips, his tough thighs, digging my fingers into the muscles on his back.

It leaves me hungry and sticky. I must use the bidet all the time. My lips are sore and worn, yet, it is like a drug, like strong hashish that fills all your limbs with a sleepy, warm fatigue—but only afterward. During it, it's another feeling.

For days on end, I am completely drugged—reduced to being just flesh which tingles when my clothes brush against my skin. On the streets, I feel him seep out of me, I look at mirror and see my lips impossibly red, and I think the whole world can tell what I have been doing with Lyosha.

Of course, it is not always like that. Sometimes he comes home, and I'm tired, I can't. I look at the ceiling, my feet chilled, and after, it is as if someone splattered an egg on my stomach: that cold, that clammy. More like visiting the bathroom to fulfill some need but it is not my need, and I grow a bit repulsed by this man with his doggy thrusts, his sorry little needs.

Mostly though, he drives me crazy. I remember the shudders and his tongue in the palm of my hand, or the pounding of his hip against mine, and I want this again and again.

Lyosha

So I got a job. Dancing. But what sort of dancing, I blush to tell you, you lovers of art and ballet. Dancing for the Cheval Rouge in Las Vegas-style numbers. Forget Toulouse-Lautrec. Nothing to do with Yvette Gilbert or Offenbach floozies in black stockings and lacy pants.

That's tourist propaganda. No. This dancing? An abortion, a bastard child of Hollywood. With a little French spice thrown in. What is it? What is this French that tourists look for? All these burgermeisters and Vikings and Texas cowboys. Chorus girls aren't even French (who have legs too short and boobs too small—except for Claudine, she's from Normandy.

Where they raise them big like cows on cheese in cold green fields. Tits like you wouldn't believe. On her.) The rest—Australians, Americans, but most are milky English girls from god knows which factory

65

town. Very working class. Can't understand their accent. Little fat hands, but legs up to their armpits and boobs like centerfolds. Don't have to dance much anyway. Just pose. In sequins and feathers.

Oh yes. The audition. Standing on stage with three hundred other dolts, slobs and homos. Limbering up, doing their stretches on the stage floor littered with dust, feathers, gum wrappers. Chatting with each other. Looking for a lay, maybe.

A skinny old boy comes out from the tables beyond the edge of the stage. Neck long like a column on the Madeleine. Inevitable scarf. Black tights. No ass to speak of. Worn off, I suppose. A wave of the hands, a clap and the stage lights explode in a harsh white deluge, blinding everyone and throwing the rest of the hall into night. Like being stuck in an aquarium. An assistant lines us up, the Master runs his hand through the few hairs he has left, and rids the crowd of cripples and uglies.

Some more claps. An invisible piano in the pit tinkles *New York, New York*. Boys stand in lines, and the master runs his fingers through the ever-thinning rug on his head. Follow his combinations that he traces for us at the edge of the stage. Outlines them for us, then turns to face us as we go through the steps. The steps were so simple. Wanted to walk off the stage. Insulting, indeed, but with only three hundred francs left, one takes few insults here and there. Flashed my crooked Soviet teeth in a smile. A clap of the hands, and he waved away half of the boys, as if they were rotten sturgeon a waiter had brought to his table.

A few more bars of music, a few more combinations and the Master dismissed another half. Seventy-five left now. For three openings.

Choreographer and our master. Outlined some slightly more difficult steps, shouting above the banging chords of the piano. Boom, five less boys, then ten less boys. And finally we were twenty left under his sharp eye.

Stood us in line again. Stared at us the way a critic stares at a new painting—leaning back on one leg, lips pursed, his fingers tapping his cheek. Four boys out. Too short, evidently. Another went, a blonde, pimply boy, but balding already and who wants a chorus boy with thinning hair? Especially one who is as prone to tears as he is, judging by the way he cried as he slumped off the stage.

With a toss of the scarf, the old boy swept off stage, to stand next to the piano in the pit, shouting out news steps, while telling the pianist to vary tempos. A few slip ups, a few poses which wavered, a stagger here, a wobble there, and we were ten.

Jean-Paul, Jean-Paul, a soprano voice sang out.

Waited there under the glaring white lights, their meat puppets. Nonchalant meat puppets, though, each as unconcerned about the auditions as if we'd just come out for the fun of it, to pass time on a dull afternoon.

From stage left, a fox-eyed woman swept towards us. Followed by the Master. One look at the diamond-pointed chin stuck up in the air and you'd have thought she was Marie Antoinette reviewing the court. Which she was in a way. Rust-colored hair, eyebrows plucked into two thin lines. Black shirt.

Asked the first boy if he spoke French; he did, and they chatted a bit like two old friends meeting in a café. Worked her way down the line, consulting our CVs and photos, pulling them out from a sheaf she carried in her left hand. The Master would interrogate the boys too, but all of us could see that she was the boss. Who might allow the old queen to pick a boy for himself, but who owned the rest of the show.

Finally, she reached me, the last line. Do I speak French? Non? Anglais? Oui?

And looking at my CV, But zeese are nothing but the ballet companies.

I have studied modern jazz, tap dancing, too.

And you're Russian.

Born. But proud Canadian citizen now.

Auditions do terrible things to my English.

You have papers?

Yes Madame. Carte de séjour. Temporary.

Very good. Please smile.

Figured it was over then. One look at my teeth, and I'd be out with the baldies, fatties and elephants.

She turned away.

Pause. Followed by a speech thanking us for audition and commending us all for our remarkable talent, and regretting the difficulty of choosing among us.

These three Jean Paul, she said, regally waving her hand, like some fucking Mme. de Sevigny, her gesture falls two others. And me, my god.

Welcome to the Cheval Rouge. Rehearsals start every weekday afternoon at 13:00 precisely. If you are late, you receive one black mark. Three marks and you are terminated. If you miss the rehearsal more than once, you are terminated. The same goes for a performance. Once you are supplied with the costumes, you must pay for damages. You must be here on hour before the show.

Congratulations again. You are all fine dancers. We are a family, and welcome to it.

Then she smiled like a barracuda.

Jean-Paul gave me a moist, questioning look, then ran along after his mistress.

Bloody fucking bitch. Bloody fucking poofter, the boy next to me said.

Absolutely, I said.

What a lot of crap about the costumes, he continued, wiping the sweat from a wrinkled forehead. Smiled and introduced himself,

Tony Blanchard.

Lyosha.

So where you from? Russia? How'd you get here?

Am wondering that myself.

Me, too. Back in Australia, hell, even in the US, we didn't have this kind of crap.

You're American?

Me? Not likely. I'm from Australia, originally. Worked in the States for a bit. Thought I'd try Europe.

Walked together to the pile of clothes and bags at stage left. He pulled out a comb to rake through the mouse-brown hair and changed his shirt.

Offer you a drink, he said, But I'm flat at the moment.

Me too.

Well, cheerio then. Till rehearsal.

Parted at the stage door. Sunlight blinding after the dark interior of black and red velvet.

Inge

Everything changes. Lyosha has his job, so we have money again; we eat normal food, meat and vegetables instead of pasta and couscous. We can go to cafés and sit with the rest of the people and we no longer have to walk and walk because we can't afford to do anything else. But we are no longer together in the same way.

We wake at noon. Noon! What would my mother say, how shocked she would be if she knew, but we do not get in until three or four o'clock in the morning.

Lyosha drinks his coffee and eats his roll. He is always quiet, with blue marks beneath his eyes, his face swollen from sleep and he dips his bread into his coffee. I notice shallow wrinkles on his forehead, spreading around the corners of his eyes, lines that surface later during the day. It is then that I realize he is ten years older than me. I try to make him talk and say something because this is the only time during the day that we have together. Also, it is quiet in the courtyard without the din of pianos and radios and children's crying that echoes the rest of the time. But Lyosha is so irritable that he refuses to say anything, or if he does, he insults my mother or me. Then he leaves with a bang of the door, sometimes forgetting to kiss me good bye.

If I am lucky and he doesn't have to rehearse, or if he cuts his class, we share a moment together in a café near his theatre. But it is only for a short time, usually with some other dancers, with Tommy, or, if we are by ourselves, Lyosha gossips about the dancers in the company whom I do not know and do not particularly care about. Then he must work, at least until on or two o'clock in the morning.

Depending on how large the crowd is, I may watch the show, but it gets old and Lyosha is only in the back of the chorus.

After work, he comes, home, or I meet him at the door. Lyosha is usually too excited to go to sleep right away, so we must go to some bar and have a few drinks. This I do not mind so much—Tommy comes along, and he is so very nice, telling jokes, or talking about his job in the United States—funny little stories. Once home, Lyosha sleeps like a dead man, completely still, without even snoring.

The rest of the time I am by myself. People say, Ah Paris, Paree, how wonderful to be young and free and to have time, what a wonderful life you must live with beauty all around you, you must be so happy. For a vacation, a weekend, yes, it must be like this, or if you are rich, with a comfortable apartment, and you speak French.

But this is how it is for me: I must walk down rue Pigalle. Pigalle where the prostitutes are out already in the early afternoon, standing by or leaning against the doors of the sex clubs with red lights, or neon couples outline against the curtained windows.

On cold days, I wonder how they can bear it; the whores who wear just a negligee or the tiniest skirts, even though they have fur coats, the coats cannot warm them. No matter how cloudy the day, there is always too much light.

The light brings out the bruises on the thighs or under the makeup. One prostitute, all dressed like a businesswoman in a navy blue skirt and jacket, always stands on the corner of rue Pigalle and rue des Martyrs. Her blonde hair is pulled back away from her square face, and her eyes behind the tortoise shell spectacles recognize me. She always recognizes me with a glare that's filled with broken glass.

Farther down the hill it is more pleasant. I pass bakeries which displays rows of napoleons, brioches, milles feuilles, tarte aux pommes behind polished windows, pastries which I cannot eat for fear that I would to be too fat for Lyosha.

I walk through Place de la Trinité and so to Place Diaghelev, ones of my favorite spots in Paris. First, because you can see the rear of the Opera rising up in gilt and green domes, a huge fairy-tale mass of a building with its busts and statues. On each side, the Galleries Lafayette draw crowds of shoppers who, unlike the mob at the Tati store, look sophisticated and elegant in their mink coats, their gold necklaces, their Italian shoes, who carry Louis Vuitton purses from which they draw their perfumes and their credit cards.

From Place Diaghelev I pass the Opera, cross the square in front of the Opera and go to the rue St. Honoré. Such a wonderful street! It is here where you find the guidebook Paris, the film Paris of great style, of fashion of elegance. Boutiques, all with famous names, line the street, names like Balenciaga, Lancome, Dior, Lanvin, Givenchy, Hermes, glitter above the polished displays. The jewelry store windows parade their sapphire rings, ruby broaches, diamond necklaces, emerald bracelets, Rolex or Phillipe Patek watches glowing on dark velvet. Perfumes, dresses, leather coats, silk scarves, luxurious wools are eyed by bronzed Parisian women.

Then I go to the Champs-Élysées and have a hamburger at the Burger King. It sounds silly, but it is not too snobbish, and for a few francs, they let you sit there for as long as you want, and you will not be bothered by some rich Arab or Italian who thinks you are there to be picked up. Because the other girls stay in the fancy cafés, and no one ever picked up a millionaire at McDonalds. There, only the unemployed boys from the suburbs may try a line on you. With them, though, it is sweet; they do not insist.

You can walk only so far and only so many times; you can stare at passersby for only so many hours and soon it becomes boring. Nothing every really happens in Paris beyond the surface nervousness and rush. Of course, you see sights, visit museums, and, if you have money and don't work at night, you may go to the Opera, to the theatre, to the ballet, to discos. It is difficult to meet people, real people I mean, not just men who want to sleep with you.

Now I stay in the apartment, reading German books I borrow from the Goethe Institut. Read after cleaning our rooms, washing Lyosha's socks, dusting the armoire and the table, while listening to the other telephones ring, the drills pounding on the street, read while hearing the sound of other people's children playing.

Lyosha

Stood with Tommy. At the zinc bar of a café on Place Blanche, cheeks to cheeks with pair of Brazilian transvestites on my left. Huge hands gave the show away. Made up pretty well though. Beyond that charming pair, the backlights bounced off the windows and the colored wheel of the *place* pulsing on the outside: the yellow headlights, the flashing neon.

So, Tommy said, why the hell are you dancing for the Cheval Rouge if you want to be do the classics?

Money. Simple as that. Money.

But I thought your mum was giving you some cash. And you had unemployment coming in from that Dutch gig, right?

Absolutely. But I have this parasite to feed.

Who, Inge? Tommy sipped his unsweetened espresso, grimaced. But she gets some money too, doesn't she? She can give lessons in German, or whatever. That shouldn't be a problem.

No, I don't want her doing that.

But you're wasting time at the Cheval. I mean, sure, you're keeping up your classes with Razumwhatsit. But you must be half-dead by now. Can't go on like that forever.

Brown spaniel eyes in a prematurely wrinkled faced. Looked with unfeigned concern, while the barman in a grease-spotted bow tie traded pleasantries about the transvestites at the far end of the bar. Or, it could have been us he talked about. Saw our reflection in the mirror. We looked like a pair of pederasts. Two boys already made up.

So what am I supposed to do?

Ahh, I dunno. Chuck the job and get on with a real company. Me, y'know, it's, dancing's just a way of getting the hell away from Adelaide and sheep-fucking-herders. But you. . .

Can't leave Inge.

So marry her and get it over with.

Marriage is for the masses. It's not for me.

So drop her and get on with your life.

Really so easy for you to say.

Then put her to work. She's a Kraut and all. She wouldn't mind.

Men go too crazy around her. They'd try anything. She already talks to strangers on the street. Even admits it to me. At home, at least, she's out of the way. No, I don't want her exposed. Some fake playboy will steal her with his money.

Happens all the time, I'm sure.

It does, though, it does, I said. Look what I did, just stole her away from her house. With nothing. Nothing. A rich guy could keep her as a mistress. Ever see those whores on the Champs Elysees? Kept women. All of them. By Arabs, or Jews. A blonde like Inge? She would make a fortune.

Okay, let's forget about Inge. You're the one who wants to be a star. And I'm telling you, you can't do it the way you're doing it now. You're just pissing about.

Listen: I have auditioned for all the companies in Paris. And in the whole of fucking France. Lyons. Bordeaux. Even fucking Rennes.

Even the modern groups? You could dance those guys right off the stage.

No, it's no good. I hate modern dance. It's all ugly. Warped bodies. You stick your ass out, stick your arm up some girl's nose. To noise. That music, is just like construction workers sawing though pipes.

It's not as bad as all that. Study a bit, then make a name for yourself with the avant-garde. Ten years later, and you'd be going strong. On the covers of magazines.

I will not dance like that. Never.

All right, Tommy said. He nodded at the shemale to my left who'd picked up a blonde man with a crew cut.

Guess they got lucky, didn't they?

He's in for a big surprise.

Maybe not, Tommy leered. They don't look like they have a very big surprise up their skirts. The he turned on his dog-like sincerity. It flooded back into his eyes. After he brushed back his brown forelock.

You must have heard from some of the companies anyway?

No. Nothing.

Nothing? That surprises me. Can't believe it really. Especially here. Frogs can't dance; everyone knows that.

Mafia.

Mafia?

Little clique. Controls everything, just like New York. They have their little groups, their little connections, networks with little stinking men running the whole show and if they don't like you pshhst—you're finished.

Maybe. But talent comes in there somewhere, mate. You know that.

What talent? Back in Moscow, I knew ten boys who could dance better than Baryshnikov or Godunov. Twenty, even. Looks, technique. Better in every way. More soul. But they're still in the Soviet Union. And these jerks, they come to the West, make their little business, and boom, like that, they get good jobs.

Godunov got the boot, though.

Absolutely. Because he wouldn't kiss the asses of the businessmen who run the show. Too honorable.

I don't know about that.

Sure. It's true. Go to the Opera Company, and you tell me, those dancers there, that they're the best. I'd laugh in your face. In deep fucking provinces of Russia—no, forget Russia,—in Canada I saw better dancers. And why is that? I'll tell you why. Connections. Pot de vin. Networks. You don't know.

He drained his brown cup, looked around the café which was filling with smoke and steam, the windows fogging over from the breaths of the patrons and the humid night outside.

We'd better be getting back, Lyosha. Curtain's in half an hour.

Inge

Lyosha, back from his class, is leaning over the sink, the skin of his back covered with goose bumps as he soaps his armpits☐ ☐. When he dries himself, he turns, and, rubbing his cheek with the tips of his fingers, asks if he should shave again.

Why shave twice in the same day?

Because we've been invited for dinner. My mother invited us to her boyfriend's place. Please, can you trim my hair?

Your mother is here? In Paris?

Her boyfriend is here. They met in New York. Now, he says, digging in the drawer of the desk, where did you put the scissors?

How long has she been here?

About two weeks.

The scissors should be in the drawer. Here, let me get them for you.

He bends over the bowl of the bidet, and I start drawing a comb through his hair and clipping the ends. Why didn't you tell me she was in Paris?

Hard to say.

Strands of his hair fall in the bowl. He keeps very still.

She only told me herself that she had arrived a few days ago. Aren't you finished yet?

How can I do a good job if you move all the time? Keep still.

Just a trim. Not too short like the last time.

But Lyosha, this is very strange. You don't meet her at the airport. She does not call you. You don't tell me she's here, and suddenly . . .

Maybe you should wear your blue dress, the one with the gold buttons.

Okay, your hair is finished. He draws himself up and looks in the mirror.

Not bad. Now, he says, where did you put my white shirt?

I change from my pants to the dress he suggested. When I turn to ask him how I look, he is already standing by the door waiting for me.

Don't worry about your makeup. You have enough and we don't have time for you to bother with it now.

We rush to the Metro, which is so packed with people we have to wedge our way in between the stinking knot of commuters crammed at the doors. We must transfer twice, at Gare St. Lazare and the Opera, again rushing down the long tubes filled with gray-faced workers going from their Monday work. By the time we reach the station for Pont Neuf, the armpits of my dress are soaked through because of the heat, even though it's winter outside. Outside of the station and on the bridge with the street lamps catching the scattered wads of paper blowing by the wind, the sweat turns clammy and icy on my skin. A woman in a fur coat passes, the hairs of her mink rippling, and I wish that I had a coat like that to wrap around my body.

At the middle of the bridge, Lyosha stops. I follow his glance to the right, to the foot lit façade of the Louvre.

What's the matter?

That's nothing, he says, nothing.

Can we go?

They think it's so great, the Louvre. You should see the Winter Palace.

Lyosha, I'm cold.

We cross the bridge, turning right at the quay, and Lyosha peers over the stone edge at the barges moored at the riverbank.

There it is.

They live on a barge?

Her boyfriend owns it. By the way, he's Iranian.

We descend the steps to the river's edge, where it must be five degrees colder. Lyosha helps me across the narrow footbridge to a house boat, knocks on a door, and a middle-aged Persian in a brown turtle-necked sweater opens the door, waving us down the three steps and cautioning us not to hit our heads on the doorway. At the moment we enter the cabin, a woman explodes, jumping up and smothering Lyosha in an avalanche of hugs, kissing him on his cheeks and his mouth, while murmuring Russian endearments. She draws back, holding Lyosha at arm's length and looks at me over his shoulder.

Isn't he beautiful? She says. Isn't he handsome?

Smiling, I nod my head. Her short nose and broad cheeks bones are like Lyosha's, but her face is topped by hair dyed yellow, fluffed out, with the dark and gray roots showing near her skull.

You do speak English? she asks, and Lyosha tells her that I do.

Very pleased, she shouts, stepping around Lyosha and extending her hand. Lyosha makes the introduction. She turns, and with a wave of her hand, she says, and this is my . . .*petit ami* Monsieur Kasra Offendi.

I turn and bump into him. He steps back, circles around and kisses me on both cheeks, beaming at me. He has a big smile, but it shows the false teeth under his bushy moustache. He disappears with our coats through a door in the rear of the room, emerging with a bottle of champagne, which he opens and pours into the glasses on the table. The air hangs heavily, the smell of his cologne mixing with the sweet perfume of Lyosha's mother. A green-shaded lamp sways slightly over the table, which is built into a nook at our side, and in the brief silence, I can hear the thump of the waves against the side of the boat.

Tenez, mademoiselle, he says.

Lyosha, sit here, on this bench, next to me, and tell me what you do. Ingrid, please to sit next to Mr. Kasra. He will like that.

You have a very nice ship, M. Offendi, I say, sliding on the bench, trying not to bump the legs of Lyosha's mother.

Merci. For me, it is a better ship because you have so kindly complemented it.

Tell to me, Lyosha, his mother says, how it is that you meet such a pretty girl. You never wrote to me about her.

She turns to me before Lyosha answers, just as I realize that Lyosha has never—ever—told his mother that we have been together. She asks if I am Swedish.

No, German.

Ah. She nods, then put her hand on Lyosha's neck.

But Mama, he says, I did write to you, you remember?

Yeees, now it comes back to me.

You are all right, aren't you? No more . . . episodes, no? Like the last time.

I am just fine. Just so cheerful and happy. Almost lobotomized, just like the doctors would like.

Lyosha, you are a fragile person.

To me she says: You knew that about him? Didn't you? He's not as tough has he likes to pretend. Very delicate boy when it comes down to it.

Mother.

Or, maybe, he's hasn't told you about

Lyosha interrupts with a waterfall of Russian.

'Madchen, warum weinest du' quotes. Mr. Kasra. Do you know that poem? He says, inclining a pockmarked cheek to me.

You speak German?

Wenig Deutsch, he answers.

Is he not an intelligent man? Lyosha's mother says. She turns back to Lyosha and begins talking to him in Russian. My eyes follow the curve of her necklace, made of piled amber beads, which leads to her enormous breasts that press into the top of the table.

She continues speaking Russian all through the dinner which Kasra serves, and she never moves a bit to help him. Mr. Kasra and I are forced to chat, with the two of them ignoring us completely.

Kasra tells me mostly about Teheran, how the Imam has ruined it, a beautiful city that used to be so decadent, the Paris of the Middle East. Now and then he pauses, covers his mouth with a napkin, and sucks noisily at a piece of lamb or a rice kernel, which wedges its way into his dentures.

After we finish dinner, he clears away the dishes and offers Lyosha a cigar.

You're not going to smoke those in here, are you? says Lyosha's mother, fluent once again.

Perhaps if I open the window? Kasra says.

Oh no. We will die of the smoke.

Okay, he says, Lyosha, would you join me outside for a cigar?

Lyosha agrees; more fuss with coats and scarves follows, then they step out.

His mother places her palms flat on the table and spreads her fingers, idly looking at the diamonds on her rings.

Isn't he a nice boy?

Yes, I think so.

But so crazy for sex.

I wait, then must ask: Lyosha?

Oh no, not Lyosha, she laughs, Kasra. She grins at me, then shifts her attention back to her fingers. I would be surprised if . . . Is the champagne finished? Yes? You'll find a bottle of cognac up there, yes, in that cabinet over the table. Please to serve me some. And for you too. No? Don't be shy, Ingrid.

Inge. Really, I don't . . .

Yes you do. There. Yes. Have you had an Persian boyfriend? No? Kasra tells me they're quite popular in Germany. The stories he tells to me about Berlin. Well. You know what they say about Nordic women. But you are not touching your drink, and here my glass is empty. More?

She pours a really brimming glassful, a la russe, she says, and drinks it all in a gulp, a la russe, she apologizes, and she fills her glass again.

I decline, wondering why she wears such a deep décolletage. She continues, a blush spreading from her neck to her cheeks, telling me about Kasra. I stop listening, wondering when Lyosha will return, both relieved and irritated that she spends the whole

89

time talking about him when one would think that she would be interested in me. After all, I'm her son's girlfriend, and maybe something more in the future.

Does he do that to you?

Sorry?

Does he—the Greek way. I wonder. You know, he was never very masculine.

Before I understand what she is saying, Lyosha and Kasra come back into the cabin.

Lyosha, she says. I want to ask you. How is the dancing?

Please. We've already talked about this during dinner. Why repeat?

But I want Kasra to know too.

It's normal, Lyosha answers, folding his arms.

But in a nightclub, Lyosha, what is that?

A job. To earn money.

Yes. I see. She puts her hand on his neck again, leans in, horribly intimate, whispering.

Lyoshinka, Mme. Razumskaya says to me that you are missing classes.

You spoke to her?

Why not? I knew her cousin in Moscow.

I work late. And we sometimes have rehearsals if show does not go well. So I miss, yes. I miss occasionally.

Her face flushes a deeper shade of red. But why take this job at all? What about the Holland company?

The season was finished.

And started again.

I am auditioning. Have auditioned.

Auditioned. Why don't they take you? I tell you why: Your technique is going. You don't work in class. Tell to me, she pleads, tell to me, why you are not being chosen?

Mama. Please. This is very boring for everyone else.

She removes her hand from him and turns to me. Smiling, So sorry to bore you. It's just my son, you know. My son only. Maybe it is better if we talk about it some other time. She continues, addressing him, What mother is not concerned about her son? It is understandable, yes?

You realize I have to eat, Lyosha says. That they do not give their filthy unemployment to foreigners?

Looking at the small square window, I wonder how often they have argued like this, the mother never moving, never yielding, a grand statue of . . .not marble, but of gelatin perhaps, something which absorbs and blunts even as it remains, soaking up the resistance.

A few flakes of snow or ash blow by the window pane.

I do not want that you should be a slave, Lyosha.

What else can I do?

Ballet, Lyosha, ballet. You are lost in nightclubs. That talent you do not have. Ballet, yes. Cabaret, no.

At this, Lyosha lets loose a waterfall of Russian, his voice rising and falling over the whole scale from low to high. To emphasize some words, he slaps the table or pounds it with his fist. Kasra retires behind the door in back; some water runs in a sink. Lyosha's mother sits, shaking her head, or nodding here and there. Now and then I hear the word Mafia, and finally he winds down, ending by glaring at the red-checked tablecloth.

Then come back to America, his mother says. You can live with me, take time, and find a good ballet company. Where you can do more than lift sluts in some pigsty.

No green card.

You lost your green card? Idiot!

More Russian rage follows, which settles into a sorrowful tone. Go to Canada, she finishes in English.

With what money?

I'll find it. I always have.

Canada, he repeats. And what is there? Nothing. I'd rather live in . . . .in. . . in. . .Deutschland.

Okay. Do it your way. Waste yourself. Suffer. Lose your talent. But, she says, gathering her anger again, never expect money from me. Stay in your Europe with your companion. Come to America, I can help you. Here I will not do anything. Now, will you let me out?

Lyosha stands, and she squeezes out from behind the table, stumbles past Lyosha and exits through the same door that Kasra used.

Let's go, Lyosha says, his face white. He thrusts my coat at me and leaps the three steps to the door.

But shouldn't we . . .

What? he seethes.

Say goodbye, thank them?

He glares at the door knob, then turns to the door at the opposite end of the cabin, and shouts, Thank you! Goodbye!

Happy? Now let's go. He opens the door and I follow him, fumbling for my scarf. I find him waiting on the cobblestones of the quay.

Bitch, he says, glaring at the glowing windows of the barge. That bitch. I don't see her for months. And first thing, she makes scandal. She should be happy I'm working at all. And the best part is it is it happens in front of you and that sonofabitch fucking Persian faggot too. She never thinks.

He digs his chin into the collar of his coat, hunches his shoulders, and turns to go up the stairs. A few snow flakes drift down, turning to slush on the pavement. The yellow headlights of cars rush past, their tires hissing. I try to look at Lyosha's face under the street lamps, to see if he is crying, but all that I can think of to comfort him with is, I love you. I'm sorry.

I'm sorry too. He cuts me off.

I can help him. His mother, she does not understand him. She is cruel. I will love him better than she ever did.

It is too late for the metro so we have to take a taxi back to the hotel. We walk the taxi stand at Pont Neuf, cold and getting colder. The lights on the monuments have been turned off. The Louvre looks dark and menacing stretched out in a long dingy pile. Lyosha keeps his hands jammed in his pockets, but I take his arm and lean against his shoulder; the droplets on his cold leather jacket cling to my cheek. The entire city, as we wait, seems frozen into a limestone dream of pompous facades, column sand domes, the ugly block of the Samaritan store squatting in the middle.

Finally, a taxi stops and takes us back to our room. Lyosha doesn't say a word, staring out the window as the buildings, squares and street lamps roll by.

Lyosha

Last chord of the piano struck, last position held relaxed. Class ended. Lungs scorched from the inside, mouth tasting of copper, sweat running down the back and into the eyes.

Mme. Razumskaya thumped her cane on the floor and called for me in that old fashioned,

95

classroom Russian of hers: Alyosha Feodorovitch, come here, please, I would like to speak with you.

One second please, Madame.

Wondered what the old bag could want. Toweled off the sweat and put on a pullover. Unhealthy to stand with sweat drying on you. Walked to where she sat on her throne, like the countess she thought she was, her moth-eaten shawl wrapped around the still-straight shoulders.

Yes, Madame?

She glanced around the studio to see that the rest of the students had finished changing. Etiquette and all. After asking the pianist to get her a cup of tea. Invited me to sit on the piano bench next to her. Winter light was kind to her raisin-puckered face, but it did catch a stray whisker growing on her ear.

I haven't much time, so I shall be brief and to the point.

Rested both her hands on the ivory knob of her cane and tilted her head back so she could look down on me even as she looked up.

Okay.

Would you be so kind as to tell me what you are doing in my class?

Excuse me?

I asked you, if you would be kind enough to tell me what you are doing in my class?

With your guidance, I am trying to perfect myself as a dancer.

Very nice, Alyosha Feodorovitch, she croaked. That being the case, I should like to know why you often fail to come here, why you are frequently tardy when you do come, and why you tend to be lazy during the class itself. She raised her hand to interrupt me. You will please notice, that I do not mention the irregularity of your payments. By comparison with the other faults, that is quite minor.

Madame, with respect, I should like to point out, if I may, that I am working and am obliged to attend rehearsals. Otherwise, my payments would be even later than they are now.

Amazed I was at how easily I slipped into this nineteenth century salon talk.

I am not interested in your excuses. Art does not allow for them. What interests me is how a man of twenty-seven can permit himself the luxury of frequent absences.

I wouldn't say that they are luxuries; rather more like necessities that are imposed on me.

You are working in a cabaret, if I understood you correctly.

Yes, Madame.

She looked to a far corner of the studio, and readjusted her grip on her cane.

What I must say to you is unpleasant, and I would not say it unless I believed that it was for the best. You are not young any more, and for a dancer that is already very bad. Even if what you pretend is true, that the dance world is made up of connections, you yourself do not have the discipline to dance leading roles. You lack technique. The rest of it—the fire, the soul—you have. That is the only reason I have delayed this conversation for as long as I have.

Under the best circumstances, you now have to settle for a second lead in most companies. But, you are growing too old already, and if I may permit myself to say it--

You may.

Too lazy. You do not work as you should. Age demands ten, twenty, a hundred times the devotion that a young man must have.

But, Nureyev. . .

Was dancing premier roles at your age and had danced those roles before.

She waited a moment, sucking on her false teeth, cheeks collapsing and puffing on either side of her bony nose.

I regret it deeply, but I am obliged to expel you from this class. I regret even more witnessing the gradual decline of your commitment. If you wish to continue classes, I can give you the name of another teacher. Upon her recommendation, I might accept you back. Until then, there is no longer room for you here.

Searched in her purse for the card of some mediocrity, some nullity of a teacher. Floor heaved and sank below the resined polish, snapping a shock up my spine, a whipcrack which racked into resolutions: To show that hag, work ten hours a day, sweat blood, wear skin to bone, burst the lungs. To become a demon of grace.

Back to the ashen light of the studio, the grey dust in the corner behind Madame's chair. A chain of slate boxes stretched out, the chain of smaller and smaller boxes, ending in obscurity in some province. With rows of snot-nosed brats in sequins taking lessons. From me. Who never exploded across a stage, alone, sheathed in light, soaring like an angel on the suspended breath of an audience, to glide back to the boards on an avalanche of applause.

Took the offered card and left.

Inge

I'm sitting in the Burger King on the Champs-Élysées. It is raining, the droplets cling to the plate glass window and, driven by the wind, merge, then slide crookedly to the bottom.

The strains a French pop song plays over the voices of the patrons and the noises of sizzling foods. Mirrored balls shatter the light as they slowly turn above the fake plants while below, at my feet, the red and blue lights buried in the floor flash on and off in their plastic boxes.

I sit quietly. If I shift suddenly or twist my head too quickly the bruises ache and my left kidney stings and something deep into the pit of my stomach flutters, sending acid into my throat. I bring the paper cup of Coca-Cola to my lips, sipping carefully, making sure that it doesn't press against my mouth because that hurts, too.

From my purse, I take my mirror and check my face; the make up covers everything. A gypsy woman passes the window, her head wrapped in a shawl; she carries a baby in her arms and holds her left hand out for money. Because she walks slowly, she stands out from the rest of the people on the wide sidewalk, and for a moment, I envy her scarves and veils. All I have is paint and makeup.

People walk by, their raincoats drawn around their necks, huddled under umbrellas.

Far up the sidewalk, a woman in a black miniskirt, a black leather coat and a blue sweater is approaching. She walks like a dancer, her narrow head held high. A gust of wind drives more drops against the wind, and the same wind opens the dancer's umbrella. It turns inside out and she turns, crouches, throws it to the ground. She turns to face the rain again, her mascara running down her face, leaving black smudges.

Lyosha

In the dressing room. Pipes like fat noodles overhead. Beige brick, and only the mirrors in their light bulb frames to show that this is someplace. A lobby for the champagne fakery upstairs, instead of a basement filled with junk.

Finished another performance for the gape-mouthed businessmen, the Japanese tourists, the Englishmen with their tongues hanging down to their bellies. Papier-mâché volcanoes erupted. Girls flashed their tits. Grinned my shark grin and danced the steps any cripple could dance. To their slimy music.

Mopped the makeup from my face, sweat drying under my arms and down my back. Boys and girls chattered away like monkeys in a zoo: Filthy wanker offered me a . . . hot as hell under those lights . . .tu l'as vue?. . .broke a strap again. . .mes mains. . hand me that will you . . . c'etait le type la-bas. . . stinks. . .dropping sequins. . .tiens . . . should take a shower. . . like someone stuck a nail in it . . .cigarettes . . . asshole stepped on my foot again. . .c'est pres de la Bastille. . .going to class . . . ta geule. . auditions at. . smoking again. . . bordelle de merde . . . get a taxi. . . j'en veux pas. . .going to buy me a. . . going down again . . .ou vas-tu?

Tommy's painted mouse face in the mirror. Wrinkles digging in at twenty-four.

Lyosha, I've been wanting to talk to you.

So, talk.

It's about Inge.

Went back to wiping my face with a towel, my skin beginning to show through grease paint.

What about her?

Hesitated, his brown eyes darted over my reflection. Turned.

Do you want a real cigarette? he asked, offering a pack of Craven As. I don't much like having to do this.

Then don't.

Do you want to go to a café, have a drink?

Maybe.

You see, Inge called me. Tommy bent in closer. She was upset about. . well, she was crying and all.

Nothing new.

Smeared some more cold creme on my face. Always reminded me of the smell of my mother's clothes, that smell.

Why don't you sit down? I said.

Girls paraded behind us. Half-plucked chickens with black and blue feathers below their shoulders.

Let them listen, I said. I don't give a shit. They find out anyway, sooner or later.

Perched delicately on the edge of the counter, he brought his face to mine.

Inge's my friend as well. Like you.

Waited for him as he struggled with his Anglo-Saxon propriety.

I think you two ought to give it a rest. Maybe you should think about leaving her alone for a bit. Let things work themselves out. Give her some room to breathe, a little space—just for a few days, and she'll be back. Inge's all right, you know, she's not a bitch. I know things are tough for you now, Lyosha, but.

What did she tell you?

Look, I saw her, right. She looked pretty bad, and it isn't good for either of you. Least, not for her. And, shit, how could you do that to her anyway? Even if it's not my business—and maybe it is my business after all—I'd like to know just how that can happen. Anyway, if you let her clear out for a few days, it seems to me that it would do you both some good.

She's not my prisoner. If she wants to go, she can. That simple.

She doesn't want to leave you entirely. Just wants some time off to think things over. C'mon, be reasonable for once in your life.

Reasonable? Fuck you and your reasonable. I love her. Why should I want to let things cool the hell off? Why should I let her go? If she wants, she goes. Reasonable. I love her, you idiot, she's my life. I give her everything.

You don't have to insult me.

And you don't see. You think everything has to be nice, with flowers, with champagne, because that's all you pederasts know about. Me, I'm not going to be told by anyone what to do about Inge. You think it's like some fucking business deal, don't you? You can look at it like a butcher weighing pig meat on a scale. Not me. Not when it's my meat that's chopped up and laid out on the paper. I love Inge. I will hold her. I will keep her. Even if it kills me.

Just so you don't kill her, you piece of shit. Listen to me . . .

No, you listen to me. I'm not an Anglo-Saxon jerk who runs away from a little pain, who thinks a little, tiny bit of trouble means everything is over. If I suffer I don't care. If I bleed my guts out, I don't care. As long as it is she who is bleeding me. I do things all the way. All the way. I love her and she stays with me. If she wants to run home to her Nazi pig fascist asshole family, she can, but she goes all the way too. Compromises. They stink like shit. You think I can live in the same city and stay away from her? No. She either loves me or she hates me. She hates me, then she can go. Not before.

Grabbed my bag, my jacket, and pounded out of that house with some of the girls and all of the boys starting at me with their stupid blank eyes.

Inge

I leave my hotel room. Even though I'm afraid of seeing Lyosha, I still have to escape that room with its bare bulb and the graffiti in Arabic. For sixty francs, that is all you can expect.

Tourist buses line both side of Boulevard Rochechouart. The stench of old grease, cooking onion, stale sausages from the sandwich stands hangs in the foggy air. Late afternoon fog. I think again about calling home from the post office to ask for money for the train. If I buy a demi-baguette—one franc 45 centimes, and espresso—three francs 50 centimes—then I can stretch the money I took from Lyosha's drawer and kill my hunger.

Mother would torture me forever, though, with her silent I was right, you were wrong seeping out of her eyes. Her dry kiss as she welcomes me home—home—would be parched from choked reproaches. Then the lectures.

I cross the boulevard to the Monoprix store, passing the booths set up for the Christmas fair. For 10 francs at the shooting gallery, you can win a stuffed bear, so of course it is jammed with short-haired soldiers on leave, potting away at the targets. One of them, with a thin, almost transparent moustache, look me in the eye for a moment too long, questioning. I leave.

Once back outside the store, I share a bench with an old woman in a black overcoat who is feeding the pigeons that flock around our feet, pecking away at the dirt. One flaps up and pokes the end of my baguette. I screech, he flies away. The Frenchwoman glares at me and mutters something harsh, something about me and not the filthy birds swarming around us.

My meal finished, I wander around the circle of Place Blanche, avoiding men's eyes so they don't assume I'm a whore. A red-cheeked tourist with a blond beard picks me out anyway, walking toward me with a map in his hand.

Excusez-moi, s'il vous plait?

I continue walking.

Bitteschoen?

So he is German. He asks directions. I tell him I don't know exactly, then wait for him to thank me and leave. He still seems to have a question; he looks at me with a doctor's stare.

Have you been in Paris a long time?

Too long.

Ah. He takes me in with his flat green eyes, but not sexually, not like a man judging a plate of food set before him.

Tell me, may I buy you a cup of coffee? Then maybe you could tell me what's worth seeing here. I pause.

Just over there, by the window. It's my first time here, and my French is not so good as it used to be. And I hate these guides and these damned tours.

Okay.

As we walk to the café, he introduces himself: he is a dentist from Hanover attending a conference. We take our seats by the window, and he asks me how I ended up in Paris. I say I'm here with my boyfriend who dances in a nightclub.

After the waiter comes, he ends the pause with some talk of the sights he has seen. As he pulls off his gloves, he notices me looking at his wedding ring and says he want to bring his family here with him next time. They usually travel to Italy—Have I been there? A shame. I really should go there. He continues to chat like this with a polite pause here and there to allow me to talk if I wish. When I don't, he begins again with talk about his son who will enter the gymnasium or his patients.

I realize how much I like the sound of his low voice, his German, how much it pleases me to relax into my own language without straining against accents or struggling with a word.

He says seeing the sights makes him hungry and asks if I would join him in some food. No. He insists. Well, maybe I will. Very good. He would been very been very embarrassed if I hadn't. He orders a jambon pays and a bottle of Beaujolais in good French.

When the food arrives, he asks me again how I like Paris.

It is very beautiful.

Yes?

But I'm tired of it. The rooms are so small. The French, they're cheap, really, and rude too for no reason. Especially if they hear you speaking German. And it's so dirty.

It's different when you live some place instead of just visiting. I remember when my wife and I went to Venice on our honeymoon. It was paradise. So later, when my practice was going well, we decided to rent an apartment there for a long vacation. Do you want some more wine? Yes? Good.

I still love Venice, but the problems we had! The plumbing didn't work, the concierge cheated us constantly, our son caught influenza from the canal water, and the grocers always cheated us with false weight.

Well, he says, stroking his beard, sometimes too little turns out to be just enough.

Then he starts telling me about the skiing trip he has planned for the Christmas holidays. As he goes on, it seems so simple to me: You love someone who speaks your own language, you like the same kinds of food, the same books and you build a life together. The husband has a good profession, even if he starts out poor, and the wife helps things along. You have friends from your hometown and your university, and they visit you in the evenings to share jokes. Pretty soon you have a child or maybe two and a real home for them.

But, he says, as much as I'm looking forward this vacation, I still envy you. To be young, and in love and in Paris.

Then I can't help it. Right there at the table, in front of a stranger, I begin to cry.

He asks me what's wrong, and it all spills out. I hardly know what I'm saying about Lyosha, about never having any money, about our fights, about my mother's never writing. My tears blur the plates, and the table.

Why don't you go home for a visit, anyway?

I can't.

Why not? Don't worry about what your mother will think. Let me tell you, I would always welcome my son back, no matter what. I can tell, just by looking at you, that your mother must care for you.

I say something about how she hates Lyosha, how I ran away without telling her where I went for a long time.

Do you want to leave?

111

Yes.

I say it just like that, as if I haven't thought about it for three nights already, hating myself for even thinking the question.

What about your mother. I'm sure she would help you.

No.

Well, here's what you can do. My conference is over at noon tomorrow. If you don't mind being around a boring old man, I can give you a ride to Cologne on my way back to Hanover. What do you think?

So, I think, it's decided. God would never give me another chance like this.

Lyosha

She'd been gone two days. Received her note, slid under the door.

First two nights: awful. Barged in on Tommy. Accused him of hiding her, called him a lot of names. He spat in my face at the end. Don't blame him. Who would? Thought of checking all the cheap fleabags in the neighborhood. But after ten hotel keepers threatened to call the police or a pimp once I got it through their thick skills that I wanted a blonde German girl, I quit.

Bought a bottle form an all-night café. To drink on the cold steps of the apartment house across from Tommy's place. It drizzled. A man tossed me a coin that I threw back. Then he spit at me before running away. My night for the gobs.

Did the all the usual things one is supposed to do. Sobbed. Cursed. Ripped the skin on my knuckles when I hit the flowers carved into the limestone of the entranceway. Stared at the wrought iron on the door I leaned against. Looked like a big spider's web. And I was just like a bug. All I wanted was some black widow to suck the goo right out of my veins. Vomited. Passed out.

Woke from having a door slam me into a corner. A witch poked her head out of the opening to tell me to leave. Reached my hand out to steady myself for the way up and put it in the middle of my own puke from the night before. Each single bone ached from the marrow out. Trudged back to our place in the dark, hoping she had come back during the night.

No. Of course not. Same perfume stuck in my nose. Ran to the hall toilet to throw up again. Didn't stop until the last drop of red bile wrung itself out of me. Slept through the day. Didn't wake until 4:30, in time for the performance. My partner said I stunk like a pig. That was all anyone said to me that night.

Bought a bottle of good old Russian vodka. Took a taxi to the apartment. Ran up the stairs, knowing if I stepped on my right foot as I hit the landing, she'd be there. Left foot, and she wasn't. Nothing in the room but stale smoke, faded perfume, old sweat, mixed with the nauseating reek of old wine.

Wrote a letter telling her all would be changed, all would be better. That her face was stamped on each of my cells, that I was too low to kiss her feet, and left that place. Couldn't stay there with her ghost haunting me.

Found a hotel room crawling with bed bugs, where the iron bed stand fit into my clenched hands, where the sink was one step away for easy puking.

The following afternoon. Suddenly. Knew she would come back, just like I know the smell of my skin. Lay on the bed, an insect dancing on my hand, and knew it. Had my own little revelation, in fact. Cleansed, washed out, transparent from the vodka.

So when I got home after dancing idiocies for the moneyed class and read her note, I thought it was a lie. A trick played by one of my cretinous partners. But they didn't have the imagination to make up a story about a sausage-eater giving her a ride gratis. And the writing was hers.

Burned the note and threw it in the bidet. Laughing. Because I had had my revelation.

Besides, her bitch of a mother would never take her back.

Inge

I stand with my bag at the entrance to my mother's apartment house. The dentist's BMW hisses away across the wet cobblestones. The Christmas tree in the vestibule glitters and shimmers with light, reminding me of holidays we used to celebrate. With my greasy hair and my makeup itching on my face, I feel more like the girls we drove past at the railway station than my proper mother's daughter. I hoist my bag, walk through the freshly painted entranceway and push the buzzer.

Who is it? rasps my mother's voice.

It's me, Inge.

Who?

Inge. Your daughter.

A long pause follows.

Please let me in.

Another, even longer pause, and the door buzzes open.

When I reach the apartment door, I try the handle. It's locked. I knock, hear a dress rustle on the other side, and suddenly my mother is standing in front of me. I want to rush into her arms, smell her good lavender scent and kiss her, but her arms are folded on her chest and her lips are one thin, pressed white line.

So, you have come home.

Yes.

Is your boyfriend with you? I don't see him.

No. I've left him.

Well, she sighs, and touches her pearl necklace, then I suppose you may come inside.

I drag my bag behind me; it bumps into a table with my mother's collection of glass swans. They fall, one shatters, she glares at me for a moment, then continues walking down the hall to the living room. I stop to pick up the broken pieces, but then I hear her telling me to leave it alone, she'll clean it up herself.

Once I'm in the living room, she asks, Why are you crying? I hope it's not over that silly glass thing.

No. Yes. I'm sorry, mother.

For the swan? Or for something else?

Her voice is like a whip. Under it all, I see what she's doing, under the pain that she made me feel for her coldness, under this disappointment for a homecoming that hasn't happened, she can manipulate me to a confession of guilt, just the way she used to do when I'd eaten some jam or forgotten to clean the kitchen. I take in this realization like air, then sob it out.

All right, Inge, this isn't necessary. You don't have to cry.

I suppose, she says, sitting down, that you need a place to stay?

Yes.

She rises from the sofa, draws me to her, presses my head into her shoulder, strokes my hair. I try to control myself, to stop crying, but when her breath catches, it sends me off again on another chain of sobs.

There, she says, you have done it to me again. Now I have to find a handkerchief. It's just like the time you and Kai played truant from school, and I didn't know where you two had gone. I called all the hospitals and police. I was desperate, worried sick, scared to death of what might have happened. Then you arrived with chocolate smeared all over your faces. I'd been very, very angry, but when I saw you there, alive, I was too happy to be angry anymore.

I sit up, pull away from her, torn. I want to lash out at her: You still treat me like a child after all I've been through, after all I have seen and done and felt, you can not see any change in me. I'm still a little girl to you.

But I can't, because I know that if I say these things, then I won't have a place to sleep. She smiles at me, her eyes far away. The lamplight exaggerates her wrinkles, the shadows making dim webs in the corners of her eyes and on her cheeks. Then I realize I have power over her. I can finally hurt her. But since I choose not to, that makes me the strong one.

Lyosha

Red-haired bitch comes up to me with a face that made her looks as if she'd just drunk sour piss. Finished my make up, rubbed my teeth with Vaseline.

118

In costume, on time, and cleaner than I'd ever been in my life from a session in the Turkish baths. To clean the scum from my pores.

I have a problem, she hissed out through her teeth.

What can that possibly be, Madame?

I have employed a drunkard who insists on showing up late and missing rehearsals. What do you think I should do? I believe you have the experience to tell me.

I'd warn him that a sadistic cunt is after him. Who is a cheap shit that wants to make him go crazy because she tortures him. By making him dance while old men jerk off under tables.

She turned white, just as they do in books.

Enough.

Her mouth popped open and shut, ready to spit out terminé. When I stood up and threw off my jacket, trying to rip the sequins off the lapels. She only narrowed her eyes. So I grabbed my shirt and ripped it open, tearing off the buttons, ripping the bow tie. Tried to hear off my pants, but they were made of some tough fabric, so I only ruined the fly.

You'll pay for that costume.

Shove it up your ass.

119

Swept up my jeans, jacket and T-shirt from where they were lying and banged out the door into the street. While I fumbled with my pants in the sleet. Started shaking. Must have taken five minutes for me to realize that I couldn't pull on my pants because I was still wearing the patent leather shoes from the costume. Took those ridiculous things off, hurled them as hard as I could against the door. Walked to my room, regretting that I hadn't spit into her face. After all, it was my turn.

Inge

After Christmas vacation, all my friends leave. Martin is in rehab for his heroin habit at the Herman Hesse School in Frankfurt. They found a replacement for me at the theater, but they promise something may open up for the next season.

No cares about me, or about my life in Paris. They just chatter on about this boyfriend, or that professor, or some movie. They'd rather talk about themselves.

Mother is already asking me to find a job at least until the entrance exams come up again. It will keep my mind off things, she says, without saying exactly what those things might be. She makes hints about this or that nice young man who is a nephew, brother, son of a Woman She Knows. These Helmuts and Klauses and Felixes show up, flatter my mother and, after hours of talk about banking, engineering and discos, slide their hands up my skirt or down my blouse.

I try not to think of Lyosha, alone in Paris. When I do, I cry, and when I cry, I have to hide in the bathroom. Mother comes, knocks□ on the door, murmurs her what is wrong and please cheer up and it will get better. At night, I do think about him, his eyes, and his back. It is like a bruise, which you can't help pressing.

My face is puffy so often that the man at the employment service sternly tells me that I should drink less and sleep more.

I am like a sailor who's been away at sea, who has endured terrible hardships, seen beautiful islands, watched his friends die of thirst, only to find that the home he dreamed of while he was away is no longer his real home. I realize then that that's the meaning behind *The Flying Dutchman*. For some, their only home is away from home.

One evening, I'm peeling potatoes in the kitchen for mother's dinner, putting the skins into the garbage. Then I see it: the blue envelope torn to shreds, hidden below the coffee grounds and cigarette butts. I dig through all the trash, put a few pieces of the letter together. It's Lyosha's handwriting. He has written me. Mother's opened it; the seal's broken.

Judas is all I can think, Judas mother who betrays me, who won't even trust me. I take the grocery money from the cookie jar, then her bankcard from her dresser drawers under her slips.

I go back the apartment and write a note telling her what I think about her and her suspicions. Then I pack my bag and take the tram to the railway station.

At the corner machine, I withdraw enough money for the ticket back to Paris. It's what she owes me for cooking and cleaning and laundry for two months.

Lyosha

A café on the corner of rue Jacob, decorated with rotten pine boughs for the Christmas season. Needles are dropping already from their fakery, their trumped-up gimcrack little religious trinkets torn from innocent trees. Needles that the gutter swept past us along with the butts and blue cigarette packs.

Mama said, If you don't have a job, that's good.

No. Not good at all. I have to eat. I have to feed Inge and me. How am I going to live? On the streets? Under the bridges?

But you're not wasting your time anymore. You're not a show dancer, you never were. You dance ballet—and ballet only. I have never understood why you took that job in the first place. And what's this about Inge? I thought that she left you.

She's coming back.

I don't think so. Not if what you told me was true.

Would I lie about beating her?

No, of course not, but she it's better that she stays away. You know, Lyosha, she's behind all the nonsense. When you met her you had a decent position. Not outstanding, but decent. Now you can simply find another job like that.

What did you do to your hair?

Why? she asked, patting it lightly with her fingertips. Don't you like the color?

No. Too brassy.

She snorted and looked out the window.

What are you going to do?

I don't know.

Then come back to Canada with me.

What for?

To be with your loving mother, for one thing, even if you don't like the color of her hair. For the work too, of course. There are a lot of good companies now. Maybe provincial, yes, it isn't the Bolshoi, but who know? You could get parts in Edmonton, say. Good dancers out there. Maybe even a few leads if you haven't ruined yourself yet. Then someone will see you. You make connections. By the way, you could always audition for Toronto again. One of their choreographers worked with Madame Razumskaya; he could put in a good word for you. Leave with me on Friday. I'll take care of everything for you.

And then rot in the sticks forever? No, thank you.

Provinces, she said, leaning across the table and bringing her face up to mine. And what's so great about Holland? Or some schlagbaum village in Germany? In Canada, you have the opportunity to dance as you should. Paris is nice, yes, I know; I like it myself, but you're not a cabaret artiste. That's why they fired you—and they were smart to fire you, in my opinion.

What about Inge?

Inge. She mouthed her name the way you taste a rotten herring, then spat it out: Inge.

What is it about that little bitch that makes you care for her so much? She's ruining you. And now, now that you have the great good fortune to be rid of her, you worry about her coming back. Are you absolutely crazy?

Thick-armed patronne looked at us as if we'd vandalized the crèche under her wilting tree. Mama followed my glance, and sat back in her chair.

Okay, she said, so you are crazy. But let me tell you—you are no damned Romeo, and you're not a saint. I am your mother and I know you too well to be taken in by your little pretensions. You stay here, and be a coward. Indulge whatever fantasy you wish. But it's me who loves you, me and not that cheap little whore you're mixed up with.

Pushed back her chair. Fumbled for her coat, her hat, her purse and her scarf, storming out on high heels that cracked like pistol shots on the floor. But in that second before she left. Went all soft, like a messy meringue as she collapsed into herself and started weeping.

Under the mud-brown eye of the patronne, I waited.

Came back, Mama did, stockings splattered, her coat buttons in the wrong holes. But she rolled towards me like a tank, armored once again. A relief. She stopped to stare me down.

There is one thing I can do for you. Even here. But it is the last bit of help you little get from me if you stay with her. Kasra said you may stay on his boat without paying rent. So you won't be left out on the streets. Which is what you deserve. You can even have your girl there. If she comes back.

She interrupted my thanks with, Until you dance, until you come to Canada, you are not my son. You are a stranger to me.

She dropped a key ring on the table.

Here are the keys. You know where it is docked. Call me when you are my son again. Good bye.

Waited, ordered a beer. Sipped it slowly. Then ordered another while the windows darkened and yellow headlights filed past.

Inge

Somehow, I take the wrong train and end up in Bonn before I realize what is happening. I can, luckily, transfer to a Paris train there, but I lose a lot of time on a trip that I wish over already, and now I'm stuck on a carriage that stops in nearly every town on the way. It snows, then, as we cross into France, the snow changes to sleet. When I press my face to the ink-black glass there is nothing but the sleet—white streaks of the drops in caught in the light of the train. A series of grumpy men share my compartment; they all have bags under their eyes, their shoulders droop. The conductor who gets on at the border tries to flirt with me, but he tries from boredom more than interest and his English isn't up to it. By the fifth or sixth ticket check, he's reduced to a weary smile that sags under his moustache.

I sleep a little, and dream a strange dream about Lyosha, something with him holding me while a clock ticks out water from its face until it rises up to our necks.

A bang from the compartment behind me wakes me, a muffled thud follows and it sounds as if someone's throwing luggage against all the walls. Sliding open the door of my compartment, I peer into the hall where two conductors are wrestling with a man in a raincoat. The man, who's quite small, must be very strong because neither of the conductors can get a grip on him. The young conductor grabs the man's tie, the man thrashes around doubly as hard, without shaking the conductor off. His face begins to turn purple, veins bulging in his neck and on his temples. He reaches for his collar, yanking it open so he can breathe. The older conductor pulls him down to the floor and pins him in the hall. A third uniformed man arrives and handcuffs him after kicking him in the ribs.

While the young conductor clears the hallway of the onlookers, the man groans on the floor, rolling from side to side. When the old conductor leans in to see if he' s seriously hurt, the man spits at him, then laughs.

Gendarmes take him off five minutes □□ later at the next station, five minutes filled with laughs and shrieks, as he struggles against the handcuffs. Then the conductor comes by to check tickets again. I ask him about the man, and the conductor says he's crazy, that's all. He has fits, but usually not so bad ones, he explains. Before I can ask him why no one looks after him, or why the crazy man is allowed travel on the train, or why they beat him, the conductor strolls away.

Crazy, that's it. That's enough of an explanation for him.

Lyosha

Moved to the boat. Only thing to do, really. And at first, it was all right. Even if it meant being the guest of my mother's syphilitic lover.

You get used to these things.

Boat was cozy. Romantic, you could honestly say, with lace curtains, coffee-colored wooden paneling, even some flowerpots with geraniums, dying geraniums but flowers nevertheless.

For a week we had a warm spell: fluffy clouds above the Seine, sunlight on the water. Stepping outside into light with the sky high above your head. Postcard perfect Île de la Cité hovered above the river. Rocked to sleep at night like babes in a cradle.

Took baths. Hot water and some Roger-Gaillet bath oil. Closed the shutters. Inge standing in the glow from the coils of the heater painted in warm, deep orange like a fire goddess. Drew a wash cloth along her back and where it sloped into her buttocks. Washed her slowly, hoping to take into my palms the pain my fists had made. She sighed, or caught her breath if I pressed too hard on a spot still sore on her ribs, her thighs or her arms.

Days, I made small presents of perfume or flowers with the money we had left. Still, we hardly spoke. Like a queen, she'd take the attentions and the gifts. Didn't complain about the cost as she used to.

Weather changed. Of course. Wind blew clouds across the chimney pots, dragged them over the towers of the Palais de Justice, clouds so thick, so low that they covered our souvenir view of the Eiffel Tower. Wind whipped the trash along the Grand Boulevards. Wind thumped big waves against the hull of the boat. Wind found its way through every chink and hole of the crate we'd landed in, and if it wasn't the wind, then the damp would seep up through the deck. Right into my bones. To stay there. Throbbing and aching in my joints. When I danced at the studio that the broke and talentless the Young Communists ran, the chill was there under my sweating skin.

Each night a recurring nightmare: I stand hip deep in gray mud looking at rows of yellow lights from apartments yelling for someone to pull me out.

Bought blankets, turned the radiator on for the whole night. Nothing helped. Chill grew teeth and gnawed until I couldn't sleep.

Inge made me see a doctor with the student health service. Cheaper that way. After waiting four more days for an appointment, a doctor gave me the verdict, looking a closely at me for the first time.

Rheumatism.

Inge

Lyosha telephones his mother, who rings M. Offendi, who promises to send his son over to look at the boat.

Maybe he knows about an apartment for us, Lyosha says, so we can get out of this floating coffin.

The son arrives the next day, tapping lightly at the door. At first, it is hard to believe he is the son of his father because he looks so different: slender, a long chiseled nose, white teeth against dark skin.

Lyosha stays seated at the table, wrapped in a blanket, huddled over a steaming cup of tea.

The son introduces himself, Hossein, and offers his hand to Lyosha, who stares at it for a moment, then shakes it.

It's really quite cold, he says in English. I'm surprised my father is having you stay here.

Me too, I'm surprised, Lyosha says.

Would you like some tea, I ask, and Hossein accepts.

He tries some questions as I busy myself with the water, but Lyosha answers with one or two words at the most. When I bring the teacup, Hossein takes off his leather gloves and sets them on the table. With his camel hair coat, his purple cashmere sweater and his carefully kept nails, he looks like a prince next to Lyosha, a prince out of *The Thousand and One Nights*.

He offers a Dunhill cigarette, which Lyosha accepts.

Take the pack, Hossein says, I'm trying to cut down.

I sit next to him. Up close, his face is quite smooth—the clothes make him seem older. He catches me looking at him and smiles back openly. It makes him seem even younger. He has been in France too long; he has a French boy's vanity.

How do you like Paris? he asks.

Not so much, I say.

That's a pity. Paris is very beautiful. Although you have probably noticed that the French hate foreigners.

There, Lyosha says, You feel that wind?

Yes. It is very drafty here.

Do you know if your father plans to seal the boat? Or is it going to stay like it is?

First, he told me to apologize for the situation.

Very nice.

Here is what he suggested: If you do not like it, he can arrange something else. If you wish, you may stay at my uncle's flat. He will be in America until spring, when he finishes his university course.

How much will this cost?

Father said to charge you the same amount as for the boat.

The same amount?

Yes. You will be expected to pay for any damages, of course. And, my father asked me to warn you about some things. It's just a studio, so it may be too small for the both of you. Also, my flat is next to it, so we may see a lot of each other. That is, he smiled, I am to check on you from time to time to make sure my uncle's goods are okay.

Lyosha stubs out his cigarette and settles his blanket around his shoulders.

Where it is, this flat?

In the sixth arrondisment.

How often would you be spying on us?

It sounds very good, I say, to take the edge of Lyosha's rudeness.

As often as you want me to.

And when will it be available?

As soon as you want. My father was thinking to rent it to some Americans, but when he heard how things were here, he changed his mind.

It has a bed?

It has everything except a toilet, which is just down the stairs. He glances at his watch, a slim gold thing.

I'm sorry to say that I have to go. I have a rendezvous. Maybe you can discuss it, and call me at five o'clock. Here is my card. Please let me know, so we can finish the arrangements.

He rises, thanks me for the tea, and collects his gloves.

Excuse me, Lyosha says, you forgot your cigarettes.

Thank you. Well, a bientôt.

As soon as he closes the door, Lyosha starts laughing.

What's so funny?

Him and his ridiculous Oxford accent. A perfect little aristocrat he is, all ready to asphyxiate old ladies in Antibes with his cologne. Ready to be a saint too—how he does his favors for us, even though it's his father who's helping us. Which only means that my mother has somehow blinded the old bastard to the money he'll lose on rent.

Do you always have to be so damn nasty? Do you have to be so rude? He comes here to offer us — you — a place to live in, so maybe your rheumatism will clear up. And he's so nice about it. But you, you the great dancer, you can't even say thank you. You prefer to sneer at him as soon as he turns his back.

Lyosha laughs, maybe this time because he knows it will make me angry. He puckers up his mouth and says,

And the way you were staring at him—as if he'd just dropped in from Buckingham Palace. It almost looked like you were falling in love with the little gigolo.

At least he doesn't stink. At least he has some manners. At least he can take care of someone else.

Lyosha snickers. Red rings pulse around the edges of my sight. I take the teapot, and smash it down on the table. It shatters, like that, with just the handle left in my hand. He stops sniggering. His eyes are so round with surprise that I start laughing.

At five o'clock, I ring Hossein to tell him that we will move that evening.

Because he had to be at his studio, forever and always at the studio, Lyosha sends me alone to meet Hossein and to fetch the keys. He told me with such irony in his face that it became a challenge: yes, if you think so much of yourself, so very much that you think it's impossible for me to notice anyone else, to want anyone else, that I am so blinded by your greatness and by my oh-so-deep passion for you that I will forever cling to you, that you own me, you possess me like you say, so thoroughly that I don't have a will of my own. If, Lyosha, you truly believe all those things, then I will show you.

You don't have all of me locked up, not quite yet.

So I wash my hair, use the bidet, paint my nails maroon. My diaphragm sits uncomfortably inside me, ready, just in case. Several minutes pass as I decide between two pairs of lingerie, the black lace and the white satin. Because I can't choose, I'll simply do without. I outline my mouth with my most crimson lipstick, slowly, pressing the scarlet cylinder to my lips. Quai Malaquais to rue de Seine to rue des Quatres Vents, the whole way I float on my perfume, under the windows gilded with the sunset, grey buildings suddenly tinged and sparkling with pink and liquid gold. I feel the eyes of men on me everywhere I pass, eyes covered with sunglasses, eyes cold blue and framed by tortoise shell glasses above an espresso, eyes that flick over me like smoke from a short fat man in a cinnamon-colored coat, small piggy eyes staring through rheum and set in liverish wrinkles, eyes that finger you almost with a touch that runs from the neck to my bottom.

Once there, I check the address, the door code. Above the entrance, a bas-relief of a fox and a crow, some Aesop fable. Instead of going straight up, I buzz the button next to Offendi. Then comes a pause, a long one, is he late? and relief with fear as the buzzer sounds. No elevator, so up the stairs feeling

137

my pulse in my wrists and throat, and there's the door.

He opens, smiles and glances behind me looking for Lyosha.

It's only me, I say. Sorry—were you expecting someone else?

Please don't apologize, and he takes my hand and leads me into the studio, saying something, murmuring, drawing me inside where the late sunlight is streaming in through the windows o the tile floor, the exposed beams, the wide bed with the blue sheets. I move closer to him, his eyes shift from me to the room, then back to me with a smile. His mouth tastes of cardamom and ever so slightly, garlic.

I had never loved a man who wasn't white. A man like him, a "colored" man, had never loved me. What a funny phrase, colored, but seeing him, the color of cloves and wood, the subtle black hairs on his arms, seeing him, as I say, against the cool blue of the sheets, or his hand on my breast makes all the other colors that I knew seem only pale, only pink, only thin as watery tea.

After, he smiles quite nicely, a full wide smile with dimples, a way he never looks with other people. Maybe . . . no, of course he's had other lovers, but this smile is for me and me alone and it thrills me to see its brilliance in the dark of our room, his whole face breaking with teeth, suddenly so like the dark children you see on the streets.

The light from our window plays on his face. It glistens on his teeth and on the suave, square gold face of his watch. A Cartier.

I like his taste in things. In cologne: Pour Monsieur, by Chanel. I discover its name because the day after our first night, I went to Galleries Lafayette, to the grand hall under the colored roof and smelled all the scents, comparing with the odor that stayed on my skin and hair.

It isn't all lovemaking. No. His family is rich. He's able to be free to do as he pleases. And it pleases him he says, to take me to the restaurants, all the restaurants, the ones that Lyosha and I passed night after hungry night, the ones at which Lyosha would snarl, at which he would laugh—those are exactly the places I ask Hossein to take me—but only when he offers—only when he insists on taking me.

We walk along the dark street, the pass into the brown entryway, the air already warm and spiced with the fragrances of the best cooking in the world and I drift into the room as if entering the soft globes of the lamps themselves, the lamps that shine like rows of tender white breasts sunk into the yellow walls, and I am warmed—just by that—in my very center. Champagne, white sweet wine and whatever it is I care to eat because with all the lovemaking I do not have to worry about gaining a gram.

Hossein just sits and smiles his public smile at me, the thin, tight one. I even order porc roti, to see if it annoys him. It does. A little, anyway. Hossein, though, orders little and eats less. He feeds on me, he says, and I am feast enough for him. His eyes wander all over me; they shape, and mold me almost as if they were his long-fingered hands, hands which will later hold me, caress me all the way from my hair to the bend of my toes.

But for now he confines himself to a soft and silent reconnaissance of the inside of my elbow or a touch just slightly too far up my thigh.

Later he will insist. Just as in the beginning, he almost forces and so I say back, no and no and no over and over again, no in the kitchen, now in the hallway after the lights on the landing have turned off, no on the sofa after Lyosha leaves the room, so many no's to arrive, finally, at yes, Because he pressed and so how cares so much when he is so kind, so ready to please and so hungry. For me.

Sometimes the waiters are very stuffy, their starched white backs glistening with disapproval. Perhaps it is racist, I don't know, but the other couples, I see this over and over—get a bit more from the waiter than the check.

But I don't care. Not as long as those gently tapering fingers with their manicured nails play on the inside of my thigh, not as long as the wine is rare, and Hossein says, of a good year, not as long as I know that, after the walk in the streets, sometimes still chilled till cool enough that the street lamps are haloed, that after the walk back to the apartment, ours or his, that there will be a time, and time again.

So I do not care, not at all.

Lyosha

Wanted to quit that bitch so badly. So badly. So: finally were out of all the hell holes. Comfortable like you would not believe in that Arab playboy's apartment. Like being a mistress, sorry, gigolo, only

141

you don't have to service the hostess. Work only a metro ride away.

Has secrets from me, she has. I know it. I know it. Little tales folded into her cunt, secreted away beneath the silk lingerie she washes in the bidet. Secrets. A man? A woman? I don't care.

Am working, am making money.

Am not so badly off.

So, I am dancing on a stage encircled by the powered glittering shoulders and the naked powdered breasts, the spotlights on and off, changing, red, scarlet, orange, blue, stark white. Light.

Betrayed again. Don't know how or with whom.

But I can smell the semen leaking out of her when I crawl in bed, bedazzled and dazed by the rushing ochre headlights. Tired.

God knows what she does.

Beginning to think I am a little like Jesus Himself, what with all these betrayals: three times before the cock crows. The semen fairly leaks out of her and it smells still under the douches and soapings over the bidet—nothing erases the stench.

That whore smell left in her hair, cigarettes and kitchens steam, herbs and mushrooms and some hint of vétiver?

Lyosha

After the Sunday evening show, I felt the pair of eyes following me on the street. Brighter in between the pools of light cast by the streetlights. Glowing in the dark.

Drilling into the back of my head, gimlets pounding themselves in.

Turned a corner, looped around a fortress of garbage cans. About face.

It. They, she, he was gone. No one after all.

Not that I actually saw them, him, her, it, no. But you can feel when someone's staring at you. In the market, at the café. On the street. A little psychic nudge and you look, then see someone's eyes and the glance shifts away. Or, they keep on staring and you and you learn why: sex, money, curiosity, then act. Or not. Nothing simpler.

So you don't have to see to know. Just feeling it is enough. Normal.

But to feel it from the back of my head to the tip of my solar plexus—that's a powerful stare. An uncommon stare, an unusual stare the difference between a mosquito tickling the hairs of your arm and a hard fast slap.

So, a strong stare. But a stare you can avoid by turning a corner and giving it—the stare, I mean—the slip.

The eyes behind me. The eyes belong to someone, yes? The eyes stare at me.

First I think it's a diseased fantasy of mine. Eyes have to be in head attached to a body. This body belongs to a person. And a person can't follow you around all the time. Besides, who would want to follow me? KGB? CIA? Ridiculous.

Someone stared at me. Maybe stalked me, Maybe someone from the audience, who someone picked me out in the middle of all the skin and sequins.

Logical, reasonable. Material reality. If I looked up from my café au lait at the bar and . . . and didn't see any likely suspects, well, so what?

If I was with Inge and suddenly a glance like two hard fingers seem to pressing hard, so hard into the back of my head, if no easy culprit can be found in the knots of people hurrying along the Boulevard St. Michel, well. That happens.

When I felt the eyes in the apartment, now that . . . disturbed me. In the apartment.

But. A peeper. Could give you the creeps like that, the stare magnified, intensified by the telescope or binoculars or even a very powerful camera lens.

This still is nothing unusual. To the girls, it happens all the time—I asked them and they all told me. Stories—about some loner who follows them around. They talk about that with quickly shifting, widened eyes.

As terrifying for them as my situation is for me.

More and longer it punctured me, that stare.

Began to wonder. Not if the stare is real. But if explanation for stare is right. Some lovesick, decrepit old man dropping handkerchiefs, tracking, setting up an apartment?

Sure, that's it.

Except that it makes me afraid, I would like the stare. But a nasty juice pumps out of my liver, pulsing in the middle of my rib cage. Makes it hard to breathe.

Yet, when the stare is away I miss it. Feel tenderness for it.

After all, it stares at me.

That's how it was for a few weeks. On. off. More off than on. Entirely plausible. Believable. Not so very strange.

But don't mistake me. Thought that I may be going insane. In the most humiliating, banal way. Became concerned for myself (someone had to).

Sudden revelation. If I think I am going crazy, then I am not going crazy. Because only lunatics think they're completely sane.

What is real? My hand, my craving for Inge's ass, the tea steaming on the table. All real.

A pair of eyes, equally real. Whoever carries those eyes would not show the face that goes with them. Not until whoever was ready. NO.

A day passed without the staring.

Then. My skinny Russian ass parked on a bench. In the Jardin du Luxembourg. Saw the gypsy hag, black and paisley shawl, ragged and stripped with shiny greasy streaks, skin the color of cheese mold, wrinkled as an old man's knuckle: a bony narrow Mother Teresa face. Thin blue lines of old ink traced tattoos: spirals, stars pointing down. Of an ugliness absolutely magnetic. Her eyes, two black tunnels into . . . nothing at all.

A real witch. Baba Yaga.

Realized then how limited my understanding had been. To look into the everyday, to search for small rational explanations for anything. What a mean and paltry, what an ordinary way to look at things. Why trust the banker, the cop, the shopkeeper for answers? How utterly fucked up.

So, God sends me this crone to remind me: keep my eyes on Him, and not to think with a bookkeeper's ledger logic. That old woman, right there, connected to the dark center, a channel to the inner blackness.

Idiot. Had thought about it all wrong, sought answers in the wrong places. Answer is not some stalker, some fictional character. Made it up so that some men from an asylum will not lock me up, no. Explanation lies in another place, the place of angels, demons, ghosts. World of insight not available to just anyone. But just as real.

Opening all around me, the garden bloomed in stiff straight rows of flaming green, black earth spitting fire in the shape of scarlet blossoms, the soaring arch of the sky capping me and everyone—

the witch, the girls in navy blue coats sailing their ships in the pool of the fountain, the men in dark suits—the sky embracing and holding us all in its blue bowl.

That's when I saw it. I am like God, or his Son. I am God.

The Eyes, that Stare, of course, belong to Satan.

Must instead radiate love, like a thousand-pointed star.

Inge

Lyosha, Lyosha, always so difficult to be with. First, he's frightened: his eyes roll like a dog's before it is to be beaten by his angry master. He peers out of the window into the courtyard, scanning all the windows as if looking for a sniper, just as he has so many times, and I ask him why once again and once again, he will not explain. He just stares at me accusingly. Does he wonder, does he know? About Hossein?

About our plans?

No.

On that day we went to the park, Lyosha, watching, staying close to the walls, just as he's been doing.

We do not talk. When he is not searching the street, the cars, the windows, doorways, cafés, his eyes are fixed on the ground. Quite funny in a way, like a broken toy with a head that won't stop bobbing.

We reach the park and sit, our eternal sitting, our never-ending, non-stop sitting.

Lyosha

World flattens. Like a drawing on a piece of glass. No depth. Figures, buildings, shapes of buses, girls, just flat.

An invisible hand tried to steals my breath. Red muscular snakes coil and uncoil below my eyelids.

Inge

We are in the Métro station at Pigalle. Lyosha, distracted, looks off the platform down the tunnel where the trains go.

We are far, far apart now. It's my fault, because of Hossein, but only I know that. Lyosha must only sense it, if he senses anything at all now. He never holds my hand, never kisses, and never makes love. Not that I especially want him to; it would only make the things to come much harder.

People crowd the platforms, and it's so hot that I am beginning to perspire, and it stinks, as usual, of city earth and urine.

Behind us, to our right, a *clochard*, a bum starts singing to himself. The words, growled and barked from the back of his throat are muffled, impossible to understand. He breaks off his song and starts to sob. And that's when I turn around. A pathetic heap of rags with two red eyes burning in the middle, a heap on the concrete gutter along the wall, not noticing or not caring about the puddles of water around him and in which he is sitting. That's when I notice the urine and deeply shitty stench, is coming from him.

He starts to weep; his tears make small clean traces on his gray cheeks. I am about to turn away when I see Lyosha. At first, I think Lyosha's looking at me because his expression, his smile, the light in his eyes, the softness of his entire face—that had

150

been for me, mine, that was the way he looked for just me and for a second, for less than it takes to breath or to sigh, it filled me up and then, as just as quickly and just as briefly, a pang as I remembered about Hossein.

But Lyosha's not looking at me. Instead, he's gazing at the howling drunk.

Lyosha

Saw a piece of bleeding earth. My father. My brother. Babe of the world, poor fetus thrown into the night.

Inge

We miss the subway.

J'ai du bon tabac, the drunk sings. Lyosha stares at him longer with that lover's gaze of his and moves, drifts to the man.

He's an even filthier mess that I realized. You never stare at people in his state. What for? It only makes you feel guilty and disgusted at the same time. You never pay attention, but now, because of Lyosha, I have to.

His feet are visible through the ragged holes in his boots. The skin is blacker than the leather, more cracked than the leather, quite as if old meat and rags had been stuffed into a rotten, torn sack. Between the top edge of his boots and his pants, you could see still more skin, pink like boiled ham, crossed with dirt, scabs, and scars. His entire crotch is wet; he must have pissed himself more than once. His tired, loose belly was caught in layers and layers of shirts, waistcoats, coats, overcoats, all the same gray-brown, all frayed, worn and tattered. He lies with his arms spread out, palms upward like a marionette cut loose from his strings. Matted gray beard, long gray hair twisted into greasy ropes as long as my forearm, an open sore in his jaw like ground meat, if ground meat oozed pus. I can't stand it any more. I turn away.

Then as I say, Lyosha glides to him, making a low, soothing sound, a lullaby. The drunkard's eyes turn to Lyosha's, expecting a few coins, perhaps, and all the while, Lyosha is cooing to him in some language: Russian, I suppose.

Lyosha pulls a handkerchief from the back pocket of his jeans and wets it under the spigot on the wall. Then he kneels in front of the man turning to him, and begins to unlace the boot. The man's trembling hand somehow makes a fist and he swings at Lyosha's face. Lyosha quickly draws his head back, seizes his wrist and leans in to embrace him. This calms the beggar, and Lyosha returns to pulling off the boot, the old man's muttering speeding up, growing louder, but he doesn't try to hit Lyosha again.

The boot off, Lyosha carefully puts it aside and starts to rub the foot—the gnarled, twisted black foot that seems more like something dug up from the ground than a part of a human body.

Taking the heel, Lyosha strokes the foot over and over, his handkerchief blackened from the first pass. The man stops babbling, truly seeing Lyosha for the first time.

Whispering to themselves, the other people in the metro station draw back, repulsed, or simply become more frigid and stone-faced as they edge away. Lyosha rises, rinses his handkerchief again, then removes the left boot and washes the left foot, with the same deliberate calm and slowness.

Two trains come and go; a few riders stare briefly on the way to the exit. The drunk gazes up at the light, passive, content as a baby in a bathtub.

Lyosha finishes washing the second foot, the removes his own jacket and unbuttons his shirt, the skin of his back terribly white, as if carved out of soap. He takes his shirt and tenderly dries the man's foot.

A policeman and policewoman warily approach Lyosha. The homeless man starts his babbling all over, loud and fast. He jerks his foot away, and Lyosha, who was bending down—why? To kiss it?—is thrown backwards, sprawling on the floor. Seeing the uniforms, the old man pushes himself up and staggers away, the policeman quickening his pace after him. The policewoman, talking into a microphone on her shirt, draws near Lyosha who lies without moving among the bits of trash, staring up at the ceiling.

Lyosha

Buzz myself in. Up the stairs. Key in the lock. Opened the door—hello—heard shifting noises somewhere below the mind, the noises you don't admit to hearing until after. Rustling sheets.

Is she sick? Asleep?

A thump. Opened the door to the bedroom. Was dark. So first, the smells: seaweed, cigarette smoke and vétiver. Figures moved in the shadows. Breathing became laughter: whose? Inge's and a man's.

Whose?

A man's.

A sudden leap of bile. Vomited my lunch, croque monsieur and café au lait, against the wall.

The laughter kept on.

I wept for this world.

I am the clown of God.

Inge

I see him over Hossein's shoulder; it is so terrifying.

He vanishes.

The worst of it is the memory of his face: frozen, white, eyes wide open, as immobile as a frozen waterfall. I After he's gone, I weep and weep.

I only laughed out of fear and craziness. It was so very ugly.

Once Lyosha goes, Hossein keeps chuckling to himself, wiping his eyes.

Classic, he says, classique.

After three days, I register Lyosha as a missing person in the police bureau.

So, it is over, finished, and a part of me is glad that he saw us, thrilled, yes, even more: ecstatic. Because it's I, finally, I am the one who can surprise and control him, that bastard who taunts me and hurts me.

Another part of me withers, dying in soft shuddering spasms that make me weep.

Neither Lyosha nor Hossein calls.

Lyosha

Took my place with the beggars.

Orders from God, direct to me. To my marrow. Left the apartment, that apartment stinking of onions and cunt, his apartment, their apartment, and began to wander.

Can't remember.

If I hold my heart as a lantern, joy shines through.

Slept under the bridge, amid the lumps of sleeping, moaning bodies, boxes and rats. Stones so hard under the newspapers

Woke. To see a young man loitering there, haloed by the street light.

Rose to meet him. He stepped back into the shadows. Followed, opening my arms to embrace him. Instead of returning the embrace, he pushed down on my shoulders and opens his pants. On my knees now I shook my head, no. This is not the vision. No, this is not how I want to serve, no. More filth.

Saw finally that I would not. Kicked hard, first in my stomach and then, as I vomited out the scraps of food I had taken from the leavings of the market, he smashed me in the face.

No.

Inge

The police call early in the morning while I am still asleep. I can't understand at first: the French, the noise on the other end of the line. Someone who speaks English takes over.

They have found a man who matches Lyosha's description.

He was discovered in the Cimetière de Montmartre. Can you describe your friend again?

I do.

It sounds like the fellow. We would like you to come to make an official identification.

Can't he say who he is? Why do you need me to do this?

Ah. The voice, so official until now, pauses, softens.

You see, there is a problem. He is, it seems, insane. Fou? Catatonique. He does not move.

If I identify him, what then?

We can either release him to you—you will need a psychiatre to register with us and sign for him. Or, he will be transferred.

Do I have to take him?

You are not legally obliged, no.

At the station, they take me to the holding cells, down a corridor lit with flourescent lights, filled with banging, telephones, radios flaring out in static and shouts. The two police stop in front of a door and indicate a small window. I have to stand on my toes to see through the glass, barred square. Lyosha sits in a blue hospital gown, the side of his face swollen, purple and yellowed around the edges of the large gauze bandage they have put on him.

He sits utterly still.

More than anything, I want to run away from there and from that figure on the edge of the bed staring up at the light. But they won't let me. I complete form after form, sitting across from a broken-nosed man who chain smokes and stares at my breasts. He's the one on the phone, he says.

When I finish, he asks me if I want to know more about how they found him.

No, not really.

It was very curious, though. You're not a little interested? I will tell you anyway. The gardien saw him around lunchtime, no umbrella—and you must remember that storm we had? He finds a particular grave, lies down, absolutely frozen. Like a statue, the gardien said, completely still. For all day in the rain.

May I go?

He reviews the forms.

They look correct. Do you wish to know where the man is going?

Please tell his mother. Her address is on the form.

But you're not interested.

No.

Very well. Would you do a service for me? I just curious about something.

What?

Can you tell me why he would choose Nijinsky's grave for this?

No.

(I see him there: his black hair drenched, the water running from his hair to forehead to chin, dripping on his white skin as he sits on the gray stone, the name in red letters behind him, the sound of rain all around.)

No?

I shake my head. He shrugs his shoulders and stares, so I must say something more.

He was just someone I met.